D1189273

BITTER CHILLS:
HOLIDAY EDITION

"*Bitter Chills: Holiday Edition*"
A horror anthology edited by Jay Alexander
Second Edition, First Printing

This edition published December 2021
by Blood Rites Horror

TRADE PAPERBACK ISBN: 978-1-915272-00-3

This book is a work of fiction and any similarities between
characters, scenes and situations in this book and those in
the real world are unintentional.

Blood Rites Horror
Norfolk, England

BITTER CHILLS: HOLIDAY EDITION
edited and illustrated by JAY ALEXANDER

with stories and material by
DENVER GRENELL, KYLE J. DURRANT, ROXIE
VOORHEES, SPENCER HAMILTON, CARLA ELIOT,
CASS OAKLEY, CHRISTOPHER BADCOCK,
CARMILLA YUGOV, JOE CLEMENTS, MARCUS
HAWKE, PATRICK WHITEHURST and MONA
KABBANI

BLOOD RITES
H O R R O R

CONTENTS

STORIES

BONUS MATERIAL

AUTHOR PROFILES

INTRODUCTION
BY JAY ALEXANDER

Some of us Spooky Folk tend to get a little depressed around November 1st. It's only natural. After all, the Halloween festivities are over; the slasher-movie marathons that, before, seemed so completely justified, are a thing of the distant past; all the bats and paper cobwebs that management put up Just For You have been taken down from the staff room; the pumpkins are slowly rotting away. And that is, if you even found the time to carve one—and if not, I guess it looks like you'll just have to wait till next year—and of course, then November will come round again, and Halloween will be over once more . . .

But some of us know, in our cold little hearts, that the fun has only just begun. So Halloween is over. So Christmas music is already playing on the radio at work. So you already feel like you're running late while everyone around you is six months into their Christmas shopping . So what? Every day is Halloween, if you know how to keep that pumpkin juice-covered tealight glowing in your soul. Nevertheless, the onslaught of Christmas is inevitable, and it'll be upon you before you know it. There's nothing that can be done to stop that jolly fat demon from crawling into your chimney, or to keep away the frostbite of the colder months . . . wait, isn't this just as horrifying as October?

Can't we *make* it just as horrifying?

This is what *Bitter Chills* is all about. You hold in your hands a work of festive horror, a means by which to keep the Halloween spirit alive and well all through the winter. Stave off that Christmas cheer with a little Christmas *fear*! If you want to keep on bingeing horror films through the Christmas season, *do it*. And if you want to take in the fantastic work of some incredible new authors, then just keep on reading.

Of course, some of the authors in this book are not so new anymore. When we first published *Bitter Chills* in February this year, it was a privilege to know that some of the stories inside were the first printed work of the author; in the past year, though, many have gone on to have more of their writing published, or written and released novels, collections and novellas all of their own. Some of the bigger names we were honoured to print have become bigger still, and it's been a pleasure to watch all of them change and grow as writers and bless us with new spooky offerings every now and then. I have to thank every one of these authors for not only taking a chance with their own work at the beginning, but for taking a chance on this book. *Bitter Chills* was the first anthology by Blood Rites Horror, and the first I'd ever edited, and it could have been an absolute failure. Indeed, there were delays, mistakes, and countless improvements made over the months that followed; but here we are now, with this second edition, and a small press that—while just as small—is still going strong thanks to these amazing people. I urge you, reader, to take a look at the author profiles at the back of the book once you're done; if you like the ghoulish Christmas gifts on offer here, then you'll love everything else they've got for you.

But for now, since you're here . . .

What you'll find in this book is enough chilling content to get you through the winter. We've got all even stories from the original edition (I'd go into those in more detail, but I've rambled on for far too long by this point, and I think it's only fair to let those authors speak for themselves). Many of those eleven have been revised or expanded, and all of them have been illustrated for your viewing pleasure. Again, I have to thank all these authors for not only putting even more work into new and extended editions of their pieces, but for allowing me to take their words and create eleven abominable drawings from them. This was a lot of fun.

But as well as that, we've got a whole sleigh-full of bonus content: with some all-new stories, poems and sequels, as well as a brand-new addition from Mona Kabbani, author of *The Bell Chime* and *Vanilla*, and an afterword from Christopher Badcock (good friend, and author of *Those You Killed* and 'Everyone to the Table' which you'll find in this book). If you're interested in discovering the twisted origins of any of these stories, check out the authors' notes included, and of course enjoy the stories themselves, many of which have become some of my personal favourites . . .

Blood Rites Horror has come a long way since *Bitter Chills*, but this has always been, and will always remain, one of my favourite releases, and I think it's certainly earned its spot as the figurehead of our little press' catalogue. I've a lot of love for this book, and for all the people involved, and I hope that you—our poor, unsuspecting readers, coming down from the high of Halloween Night—can find some distress and agony in its pages this Christmas season. Never mind the yellow snow; avoid the red . . .

Jay Alexander
November 1st, 2021

CONTENT WARNING

Please be aware that many of the stories in this book contain graphic and violent content, as well as strong language and unsavoury or potentially triggering imagery.

A full list of content warnings can be found at the very back of the book. Please refer to this for any potential triggers, but be aware of spoilers.

STORIES

THE BURNING BOY

DENVER GRENELL

THE BURNING BOY
BY DENVER GRENELL

I was sixteen years old when the burning boy first came to visit.

It was the beginning of winter, and the snow had come early, covering the land in a frigid blanket of white. Winter was always my favourite season. For me, the sensory smorgasbord it provided far outweighed the hardships of the cooler months. Even now, as a thirty-two-year-old man, I ll stand outside on a winter s morning and inhale the air and savour the smells. The pleasing aroma of my morning coffee mingled with wood smoke and a hint of petrol fumes released by flooded car motors as commuters struggled to start their cold vehicles.

The day the burning boy appeared, I came home just as the sun began to retreat below the horizon, making way for the night to sweep in and wrap the town in its black embrace. After completing my evening chores of chopping firewood and lighting the fire, I sat in my upstairs bedroom, pretending to write an assignment on *King Lear* and waiting for the call that dinner was ready. My tired mind swam with thous , thoths , and howls of madness' in some bloody storm. It had taken me ten minutes to read just one page of the antiquated tosh. I dropped the weighty volume of Will s *Collected Works* on my desk in frustration, the impact almost knocking over my glass of cola.

It was then that I noticed a bright orange glow flickering in the gloom outside. I squinted out the window. A bright light danced there in the darkness. At first, I thought it was someone carrying a lantern through the trees that lined the western side of our house. But that notion was quickly dispelled when the figure came into focus.

The burning boy stood at the edge of the snow-covered woods, a black figure cloaked in a blazing shroud of fire. A funnel of thick, black smoke rose from his body, billowing through the trees, another chimney expelling its fumes into the bitter night. The heat of the fire melted a perfect circle in the snow around him. His eyes radiated white-hot light, and they were looking straight at me.

I tried telling myself that some prankster must have lit a mannequin on fire for a lark. If it were anyone, it would be those cheeky pricks, Davey and Callum, trying to put the shits up me. I scanned the trees, hoping to spy the culprits. Perhaps they were hiding in the forest and any minute they would burst forth and point up at me while laughing hysterically.

That s when the burning boy waved his fiery hand at me. I yelped with alarm. My right arm shot out, knocking over my glass of Coke, soaking the textbook with brown liquid.

Though I was terrified, I can t say I was surprised to see this fiery wraith emerge from the black forest. I knew who the burning boy was. And I was there a year ago on the night he died in the fire.

His name was Martin Coverdale. Marty to his friends, of which there were few. He was a bit of a lone wolf—a long-haired delinquent type who preferred to exist on the periphery of the school s social circles, dipping in and out when he felt like it. He and his mother moved around a lot after his father left. I got the sense that by the time they settled in Templestowe, Martin was content to float through the wide-open sea of teenage life, a lone buoy amongst the flotsam and jetsam, just waiting for the current to carry him on to the next port. He wasn t exactly a friend, but sometimes he d kick around with my group of guys, given our shared enthusiasm for heavy metal, 2000AD comics and weed. November fifth last year was one such occasion. Guy Fawkes Night.

Me, Davey Hetherington, Callum Chapman, and Martin had taken three bags of fireworks, two bottles of my Dad s homebrew, a baggy of weed, and a petrol can deep into the woods behind my house. We followed the well-worn bike track for a while and then at a certain juncture, veered off onto a less-travelled path, but one every self-respecting teenager knew well. Young people need a sanctuary from the mundanity of the everyday, away from their parents, teachers, and police. In our small unremarkable town, we had the quarry.

Jamie. Puff of the good shit?' Callum handed me an oversized joint as we strolled among the narrow copse of trees. Pine needles crunched beneath our feet as we exhaled the pungent smoke into the cooling air. After a while, the trees began to thin as the land rose to meet the foothills. The thick beard of pine trees was replaced by the patchy whiskers of gorse and scrub. The soft dirt underfoot became hard clay as we neared the old Somerset Quarry. The perfect place for a Guy Fawkes bonfire.

The quarry had been abandoned since the recession in the early 90s wiped out a lot of the local industry in Templestowe. The only hint of its former glory was the battered remains of an old shed, formerly the smoke room, which had been reduced to a rusted steel frame. Pieces of rotten wood clung to the structure like flesh on a skeleton that had been picked at by birds. There was little chance of our bonfire spreading to the trees from here. And best of all, there wasn't a goddamned soul to ring the police or fire brigade on us.

The quarry itself had a circumference of about a kilometre all around the base. Rising on three sides were steep walls of rock and clay, creating three-quarters of an amphitheatre. Large piles of earth sat in bulbous clumps at the bottom of the walls, sinister reminders of the instability of the terrain.

We d first come to the quarry when we were seven years old. Davey s dad was a site foreman up there, so he d taken us up there for a tour. On the weekends, the boys would come to my house, and we d sneak away to the quarry. If it was quiet, we d run around playing war games with tree branches for guns. Sometimes I liked to imagine I was a gladiator, strolling out into a coliseum in front of thousands of cheering Romans, ready to do battle.

Now it was just a disused quarry, devoid of the fanciful inventions of a pre-pubescent mind. A few years after it closed, we ventured back up there to smoke cigarettes and read Playboy mags. Now we came here to drink, get high, and talk the sort of shit teenagers talk about—heavy metal, horror movies, and girls. We d tried to convince some of the girls from school to come up here with us, with little success. There was one time when Tracy Williams and a couple of her friends agreed, but it pissed down with rain, and they quickly left, not seeing the appeal of hanging out in a cold, wet quarry with three stoned, horny guys. Can t say I blame them really.

Martin had tagged along because I d let it slip that we were going to have a bonfire in the quarry. We d been talking during gym, and he d asked me what our shitty little town did for Guy Fawkes. Martins eyes lit up at the mention of the bonfire, and he had quickly offered to make a Guy. As we hadn t thought to make one ourselves, we agreed to let him tag along. He had shown up at my house with his creation, which consisted of a pair of moth-eaten overalls, stuffed full of newspaper and twigs. A polystyrene mannequin head with a hideous painted face sat atop the lumpy body, staring at us with lifeless eyes.

The week before Guy Fawkes, we had carried branches and bags of kindling from the edge of the forest up into the quarry. Because of our efforts, we had enough wood for a formidable bonfire. Before long, we had fashioned a jagged wooden pyramid and in the waning light, we admired its twisted, natural beauty. To my stoned mind, which was teetering on the paranoid end of the scale, the gnarled structure resembled a giant pile of bones—a funeral pyre. I shuddered. A healthy dose of alcohol was what I needed to take the edge off my paranoia. I beckoned to Davey, who strutted cockily around the heap, swigging from a bottle of frothy homebrew.

Hey Dee, give us a swill?'

Davey grinned his dopey grin and handed me the bottle. The cool liquid entered my throat, the familiar bitter taste easing my mind almost instantly.

The sun began to dip, plunging the quarry into a quickening gloom. An arctic chill descended upon us. I buttoned up my duffle coat and watched my breath wisp from my mouth. It s your spirit escaping, my overactive mind thought. Soon you will have none left. Once again, I banished the dark thoughts with a comforting gulp of beer.

With the Guy slung over his shoulder, Martin scaled the wooden construction with awkward enthusiasm. He placed the Guy at the pinnacle of the heap, leaning its sagging torso against the branches. Meanwhile, Davey had begun dowsing the base of the pyre with the can of petrol he d borrowed from his dad s garage.

Davey, ease up man, I m still up here,' Martin growled from the top of the pyre, as he struggled to right the non-compliant Guy.

All right Marty, don't shit your pants,' Davey sneered, as the last of the petrol drained from the can.

Callum rummaged in one of the bags of fireworks and pulled out a large Roman Candle, the kind that shot multi-coloured fireballs into the air. He placed the firework on the hard clay ground a good ten metres distance from the bonfire. Crouching down, he flicked his Zippo lighter to ignite the candle s wick. Sparks fell from the top of the firecracker, a small precursor to the imminent explosion. Callum rose and started jogging on the spot with anticipation as the Roman Candle hissed like a cornered snake.

Not yet, you fuckwit,' Marty cried from the top of the wooden heap. There was panic in his voice as he struggled to climb down the far side of the pyre.

Hurry up, Marty,' an unconcerned Callum laughed. Shit is about to get hot!' He didn t even look up to see if Marty had reached a safe distance when the firework erupted.

Yeah, baby!' Callum hollered, as the orange ball arced upwards, curving through the air. The light from the firework illuminated our pale faces and cast flickering shadows along the walls of the quarry. The look of manic joy vanished from Callum s face when he saw the trajectory of the fireball. For an agonisingly long moment, we watched in silence as the ball reached the apex of its journey and started to drop towards the edge of the pyre.

Marty, get out of there,' I roared as the petrol-soaked wood erupted. Martin tried to hurl himself off the burning pile but he rolled a metre and became lodged between the branches.

Help me!' Thick smoke rose around him, and within seconds he was enveloped by the hungry flames.

Water! Get the fucking water!' Davey shrieked at me.

I grappled with my bag, pulling out the water bottle I d packed earlier. It was mainly to quench the dry throat I get from weed, not to put out a raging bonfire. The roar of the blaze and Marty s high-pitched screams merged into a phantasmal choir, echoing off the walls of the quarry. We scrambled around the pile to see Marty s arms reaching out of the inferno.

I tore the lid off the bottle and hurled the liquid onto the fire. The pitiful amount of water did nothing to halt the inferno. The fire roared mockingly—*You can t stop me from feeding. I am hungry.* The flames were too thick. Martin went silent. His arms dropped limply into the flames, the blackened skin peeling back to reveal the red meat beneath. We stood there in stunned silence, our distraught faces bathed in the orange light of Martin s deathbed. It was a funeral pyre.

Wh-what do we do?' Callum stared at me with the wide, frightened eyes of a child much younger than sixteen. I saw two tiny bonfires burning at the centre of each of his pupils. I couldn t speak. This couldn t be real. It was only meant to be a bit of drunken fun up in the hills with some mates.

I m getting the fuck out of here,' said Davey coolly, turning away from the fire.

Affronted by his callous indifference, my voice came back from the cave it had retreated into. You fucking asshole! What about Marty?' I spluttered. The thick smoke filled my nostrils. Coughing, I went and stood in Davey s path, despite being smaller than him.

What about him? Dude s fucking cooked!' Davey shoved past me roughly. He picked up the fuel can and retreated down the hill.

It was his own dumb fault!' he yelled back at me.

He s right, Jamie. He shouldn't have been up there!' Callum seemed anxious for me to validate his and Davey s swift dismissal of Marty s death.

And you shouldn't have lit that fucking firework while he was up there! We can t leave him here! He s a mate.'

He s not my mate. You invited him up here, not me!' Callum glared at me with accusing eyes. Then he grabbed the bag of fireworks and followed Davey down the hill like

21

a disobedient dog who fears a beating from its master.

I dropped to my knees. Tears streamed down my hot, red cheeks. Marty! I m sorry! I m so sorry.' I pressed my face into the cool, damp ground, hoping to burrow into the muck and marrow once and for all and take Marty s place if it was possible to offer myself instead of him. It was our fault. Ours.

Once the others had disappeared, I returned to the fire. The winter chill had infected my bones, and the blaze offered a warm respite. Sitting cross-legged, I stared solemnly into the yellow heart of the bonfire. I remained there until it had burnt down to a smoking husk. Marty s charred skeleton lay before me, curled up within the ashes, like one of those frozen bodies from Pompeii.

I decided that his bones needed to be buried right here in the quarry where he died. I don t know what compelled this course of action—I wasn t consciously acting out of self-preservation—it just seemed right somehow. I doused the embers with handfuls of damp dirt. When it had cooled, I removed my sweater and wrapped it around my hands. Carefully, I pulled the remains of Martin Coverdale from the charcoal, bone by steaming bone.

Burrowing my hands into the soft earth and clay, I dug and dug until I d made a deep, oval-shaped hole. I pushed his remains into the roughly hewn grave, weeping and apologising over and over again. Once I had filled the hole in, I bent over in the dirt and prayed for forgiveness. My tears mixed with the damp earth. I imagined them soaking into Marty s grave and further cooling his warm bones. Standing up, I looked at his resting place for a final time. I m sorry, Marty, you deserved better than this.'

I staggered down the hill on weak legs and into the dark forest. At one point on the return journey, I stopped and leaned against a tree so I could vomit into the damp pine needles, my bile joined by another flood of bitter tears.

The burning figure outside my window stood staring up at me. Staring and smiling. A jagged, yellow semicircle curled upwards where his mouth should be, leering at me with his sinister Cheshire cat grin. Then, he turned and disappeared into the forest. Martin, the burning boy, was gone. I sat there, rigid with fear. Cold dampness seeped into my crotch. Jesus, had I pissed myself? I looked down and realised the spilled cola was dripping onto my lap. I grabbed a towel off my wardrobe door and mopped up the liquid, first from my crotch and then from the brown-stained Shakespeare book.

There was a rapping on my bedroom door. I lurched up from my chair in alarm to see my mother's face peering at me from around the door.

Sorry hun, didn t mean to scare you. Dinner s ready.' She flashed me a smile and then departed, blissfully unaware of the terrifying visitation that had just taken place.

I ll be there in a sec,' I replied weakly. I felt ill, just as I had on that night one year ago. My stomach knotted up, threatening to void itself all over my homework. I hastily opened my bedroom window in case it decided to do just that. The cold air blasted me in the face and calmed my churning innards. I breathed deeply, hoping to smell those familiar winter odours. But instead, I smelled petrol, smoke, and burnt meat. I threw up all over my already-sodden book.

Once my stomach settled, I wrapped the vomit-covered book up in the damp towel and threw it in the bag-lined rubbish bin beside my desk. I tied the ends of the bag off and lobbed the foul bundle out of the window. It dropped into the snow, where it would lie until tomorrow when I could dispose of it in the woods. I dared not venture out tonight, for fear of Martin returning to take me away with him, back to whatever hellish realm he called home now.

The sound of exploding fireworks in the distance broke the silence, as if to remind me it was Guy Fawkes night. Admittedly, I had tried to block the date from my mind. All week long, I had thrown myself into homework, reading, guitar practice—anything to take my mind off this dark anniversary. There had been no discussion of it between Davey, Callum, and me at school in the previous days. No words at all in fact. Just silence and a solemn, fearful look shared between the three of us.

*

After Martin s death, we decided not to tell anyone. And by we, I mean that Davey decided that for us. In fact, his exact words were: If you tell anyone, I ll burn your fucking houses down.' He said it with such menace that I actually believed him. Predictably, Callum agreed. Outnumbered, I reluctantly gave in to his threats. Davey had always been the unspoken leader of our group and quick to anger, but he d never threatened us like that before.

I drifted apart from the other two after that. Callum still followed Davey around like the obedient puppy he was, but I retreated into other activities. I practised my guitar as if my life depended on it. I had only been playing for a couple of years, but I threw myself into it with a renewed fervour. I sat in my bedroom and practised guitar scales and riffs until my fingers blistered. The busier I was, the less time I had to think about Marty, and consequently, the less I heard the echoes of his screams in the darkness as I lay in bed at night.

Fortunately for us, no one knew Marty had been hanging out with us on Guy Fawkes night. He lived with his mother, Dolores, who worked at a local bar in the evenings, which afforded him the enviable freedom to come and go from home as he pleased. Because of this, we managed to remain relatively free from suspicion. Dolores didn t know where her son had been that night. The police came to school and questioned everyone, but no one knew anything. There had been another Guy Fawkes party that night at Tracy Williams house, and the three of us claimed we were there and never saw Martin Coverdale at all, a sentiment corroborated by most of the kids in our year, who in their inebriated states wouldn t have remembered if we were there or not. The three of us also did a pretty convincing job at projecting vague teenage apathy during the questioning to hide the guilt that churned within us.

Martin s mother Dolores told the police he had threatened to run away from home many times. The night before Guy Fawkes, they had fought—a not uncommon scenario in the Coverdale household according to their neighbours—and he had loudly announced he was going to do just that.

In the end, with no evidence to support foul play, it was decided that running away from home was the most likely answer. Dolores had no idea where her ex-husband even lived anymore. The police apparently followed up a few family contacts but came back with nothing. The case remained open, but with no evidence to go on, it stagnated, then stalled altogether. It was just another missing person's case in a filing cabinet filled with similarly sad stories.

A few months later, I saw Marty s mother, looking worse for wear, wandering down our street with her dog. As she walked, she stared vacantly at the houses as if looking for her missing son, clearly not content with the general consensus that he had run away from home. A crushing wave of guilt and sadness overwhelmed me, and I almost got up and ran into the street to tell her what had happened. But I didn t. I stayed in my seat and watched her from my bedroom window as she walked by, a lonely shadow, like her son but instead of flames, she was engulfed in grief.

Now, as I sat there in the same chair, having just seen Marty s flaming effigy wave at me, those same waves of guilt came flooding back. I reached for the phone and dialled Davey s cell. The call just rang out. I hung up and tried Callum s home number.

Who is it?' Callum s voice was cracked and breaking.

Callum, it s Jamie.'

Jamie! Fuck, man, I was going to call you. I think someone knows what we did.'

What do you mean?'

I mean there s a burning fucking mannequin outside my house. It s there right now!'

Listen to me. I saw it too. But it isn t a mannequin. It s him!' The words sounded ludicrous as I spoke them, but it didn t make them any less true. It s Martin!'

Fuck off! If you and Davey have set this up, I m going to kill youse!' he spat down the phone line. There was a pause. Oh shit!'

What is it? What s happening?'

It s walking now. It s walking towards my fucking house!' Panic and fear radiated from the phone.

It s Martin! He—I think he wants us to make amends!' I pleaded. The thought had barely formed in my mind before I blurted it out. I know it sounds crazy, but tell him

27

you re sorry.'

Marty got himself stuck in that bonfire. It had nothing to do with me!' Callum shouted back at me. Shit Jamie, he s right outside!'

Callum. Call the fire brigade. Then get the fuck out of the house. I ll be there in a few minutes!' I threw on a thick jacket and raced down the stairs two at a time.

Jamie! Where are you going? It s dinnertime.' Both of my parents were seated at the dining table, staring at me with their well-practiced looks of disapproval.

'Out!' I flew through the front door into the crisp night air before they could protest further.

It was closer to ten minutes to Callum s house, and I was panting heavily and drenched in sweat by the time I d ridden the five blocks on my ten-speed. As I neared his street, I could hear sirens ringing out, singing their urgent songs of alarm.

I smelled the smoke before I saw it. As I turned into Callum s street, I saw the thick dark plumes spiralling upwards like a black tornado. Flames belched outwards from his bedroom window, licking the night air. There was a crowd of distraught people standing in front of the house backlit by the inferno, which made them resemble a small forest of trees being threatened by an unruly bushfire. As I got closer, I saw neighbours restraining a flailing Mr. Chapman from entering his own burning house. An inconsolable Mrs. Chapman sat weeping on the front lawn.

I dropped my bike on the road and fell to my knees. I was too late.

At that moment the wind changed direction and the smoke was carried towards me, seeking me out. It had the familiar stench of burnt flesh and wood that I first smelled a year ago and again earlier tonight. My already tender stomach heaved once more. I dove onto the frosty grass strip that lay beyond the footpath. The cold blades of grass crunched under my hands. They felt like hundreds of tiny knives, pressing into my palms. I retched, but nothing came up, my stomach still empty from its previous purge. Mucus and tears congealed on my top lip. Despite being surrounded by houses and people, I felt as though I was back in the quarry, alone, watching Marty burn all over again.

I now knew that Martin had come back for us. To make us pay. Was I to be next? He had already visited me tonight. He had waved and smiled even. Was that a warning of my impending fiery death or was he gratefully acknowledging the last rites I performed for him a year ago today?

The following week was a sombre affair. I attended Callum's funeral with my parents. In complete contrast to the blazing heat of the fire which claimed him, Callum s memorial service was held on a bitterly cold day. The morning s frost was still lingering at midday when we all filed solemnly into Templestowe Cemetery. The sun hid behind an expanse of grey cloud, which seemed intent on trapping the frigid air beneath it for as long as it could.

The assembled mourners shivered their way through the ceremony, the steam from their mouths resembling the smoke rising from Callum s burning house—and Martin s pyre.

The investigation into the fire concluded that Callum had fallen asleep with candles burning in his room. An autopsy confirmed that he had been smoking marijuana—of course, he had, he smoked it every other day. In the weeks that followed, there was a renewed zeal for the mostly forgotten D.A.R.E. anti-drug initiative. This revival was spearheaded by the local Anglican Church Youth Group. Callum s grieving parents, who were looking for something to blame for their loss, became the solemn faces of the campaign. There were rallies. Petitions. Pamphlets stuffed into letterboxes.

A few days after Callum's funeral, I confronted Davey in the school car park. I wanted to tell him about what really happened to Callum and warn him that it was probably going to happen to us at some point as well. Davey being Davey, refused to listen, told me to fuck off, then shoved me roughly to the ground and promptly left. Texts and phone calls were ignored. He changed his email address. From then on he ignored me at school, sometimes even ducking out of classes quickly to avoid any contact. A few months later he dropped out altogether and got a job, driving a supermarket delivery truck between the towns across the county. I didn t see him again after that. It was almost as if he had already been claimed by Martin and extinguished from existence.

Once again, life eased back into a numb sense of normality. I focused on my schoolwork and music. Our band entered the regional Battle of the Bands competition, making it to the finals where we won the Best Stage Act award, which is a nice way of saying that we sounded like shit but put on a good show. Although I found contentment in these pursuits, there was the ever-present threat of death looming in the background, waiting for the right moment to pounce and claim its deserving victim. The music I was writing became darker, heavier. Songs that had previously sounded like early Metallica now edged into the realm of Doom metal, a literal aural expression of my state of mind.

Another year went by. The cold apparition of winter returned and before I knew it, Guy Fawkes night once again reared its ugly, flaming head. My parents thought it odd that I didn't want to go to any Guy Fawkes celebrations, preferring to stay home and do homework instead —just like last year.

And just like last year, I sat upstairs at my desk overlooking our backyard. I tried to play guitar but my fingers wouldn't work properly. My mind was focused on what I d come to call the Dark Anniversary. I sat upright in my chair, my eyes trained on the edge of the forest. Every so often there was the intermittent hiss and pop of fireworks letting off in the distance.

I hadn t eaten anything all day and around 6 p.m. my

stomach began to groan with hunger. My knees creaked as I stood up from my seat. I realised I had been sitting there without moving for two hours. I stretched my arms upward in a V, allowing the blood to flow back to my numb limbs. And that was when I saw the familiar flickering of light amongst the trees. My spine tightened and a lightning bolt of fear jolted through my body. I began to sweat, almost in anticipation of the fiery death that was surely coming for me.

Martin, the burning boy, emerged from the trees and stood in the exact same spot he had one year ago. Again, he smiled. Again, he waved. Again, he turned and walked away.

I exhaled loudly. I had been holding my breath the whole time he was there—maybe a minute or so. I slumped back into my chair. Although there was no guarantee, it seemed like I had been spared for another year.

My phone rang. I jumped. I knew who it was before I answered the call.

Jamie! Fuck! He s here! He s here, man! Marty!'

Davey, slow down. I just saw him too. Look man, you need to face him. Make amends.'

Make amends? What for? It was Callum that did it. Not me, man! Why s he after me?'

I went to answer him, but there was a flurry of swearwords and then he hung up. I tried his cell again, but it just rang out. I called the landline at his parents' house. His mother answered.

Oh, hi, Jamie. How are you? We haven't seen you since, well, since the—'

I m sorry, Mrs. Hetherington. It s urgent. Is Davey there?'

She seemed taken aback by my haste. Well Jamie, you just missed him. He left in a bit of a hurry. If you tried his cell—'

I hung up and dialled 999.

Yes, my friend is in trouble. His name is Davey Hetherington. He rang and told me someone was after him. He sounded really scared. Yes . . . ' I gave the police as much info as I could—home address, cell phone, vehicle—and left it at that. It was between Davey and Martin now. I hoped like hell he took what I said to heart. I had no idea if repenting in front of Martin would make any difference, but it was all I had.

Three hours later, the police cruiser pulled up outside my house. Davey s car had been found on one of the backroads north of town. It appeared he was going too fast, got into a skid, and veered off into the thick trees that lined the road. Apparently, the fuel tank had caught fire and the car had been burned to a blackened metallic husk. Some of the surrounding trees had also caught alight but the fire department had been able to contain the blaze before it could spread.

At Davey s autopsy, the coroner found he had a blood-alcohol level of .150. And although they noted the fact he died on the anniversary of his friend Callum Chapman s death, ultimately it was seen as a tragic coincidence. A young man commemorates his friend's death with half a bottle of whiskey and then goes driving in wintry conditions. Case closed.

Now the burning boy only had one victim left to claim.

I ll never know for sure why Marty kept sparing my life, but I can only surmise it was because of the burial I gave him in the quarry. The tears of remorse I shed over his grave.

Even now, many years later, the burning boy returns to visit me every Guy Fawkes night. And every year he takes one step forward. Every year, Martin gets closer to my front door. Every year, he watches me with his yellow eyes. He waves his fiery hand. He grins his orange grin. And I look back, watching. And waiting.

SNOWBLIND

KYLE J. DURRANT

SNOWBLIND
BY KYLE J. DURRANT

Under reasonable circumstances, Neil would have been happy to stay in the car. It served well as a shell of security, after all, offering warmth and safety; it provided a barrier from the elements, and from people, and he always had his Pink Floyd CDs at the ready to drown out the blaring horns of traffic and the shouts of impatient drivers. When the weather got unpleasant, he could simply sit fast and wait for it to pass, untouched by the cold and wet.

Unfortunately for Neil, these were not reasonable circumstances.

First had come the snow, drifting down from a gunmetal grey sky in friendly flurries, flitting past the window like fairies. The hillside road had been mercifully dry, and it seemed the drive would continue to be safe; Neil turned up the heating a fraction.

Soon enough, though, a steady, sweeping wind joined the snow, bringing with it thicker, heavier flakes that struck the windscreen like cotton bullets. Vision became obscured, the grey sky descending, snow melting onto the road. The wipers sped up, fighting against a gathering blanket of white. Neil knew he should slow down, but impatience tempered his caution, and he maintained his speed.

Icy cold seeped into the car, ignoring the efforts of the heater, setting a chill into Neil's fingers. Tiny jolts of needlepoint pain danced along his skin every time he adjusted the steering wheel. He whacked the heating up to full, but the chill would not be chased away.

Snow flew past like little lances of light, reflecting his headlights, brighter than the darkness that now enveloped the road. Whistling wind clawed at the seams of the doors, buffeting the car, shaking it as Neil manoeuvred along the winding road. He considered stopping—he could pull over and wait for the storm to pass—but realised that by the time another car saw him it would be too late to stop. Part of him could already hear the crashing of metal and glass as his body was crushed. A shiver ran through him, oddly unconnected to the icy swirl outside. No, his best option was to keep pushing forward, he decided. In another twenty minutes or so he would be home, back in the warmth with his wife.

She'd be worrying about him, no doubt. If the snowstorm was swallowing him here, it seemed likely his house was at least on the edge of its assault. A few strong gusts of wind and some thick flakes of snow would have her pacing back and forth in front of the window until he finally pulled into the driveway.

'Hey Siri,' he said; the phone lit up. 'Call Deborah.'

As the phone rang, the blizzard upped its intensity, wrapping the car in a dark shroud of ice, the headlights becoming increasingly obsolete. Neil squinted at the road ahead, barely able to identify the dividing lines on the asphalt.

'Hi, honey,' his wife's voice buzzed over the speakers. The sound quality wasn't great; the storm must have been interfering with the signal. 'Everything okay? The weather isn't looking too good out there.'

'I'm on my way,' Neil replied. 'It's not great, no, but I'm taking it as easy as I can. Shouldn't take me any more than . . . hm . . . twenty minutes, I guess.'

'You can take thirty minutes to get back if it means you're driving safe,' she said. There was a slight catch to her voice, betraying her worry. 'The wind is rattling all the windows; it could push you off the road.'

Neil almost laughed. 'Don't worry about a thing, I'll be home soon, I promise. If we're lucky we'll get snowed in, and I won't have to—'

It crept up on him, taking full advantage of his unfocused mind. First the front right tyre struck ice, the car sliding into the oncoming lane, and then a violent gust of wind swept down from the hill on his left, striking the car with full force. Neil released a shocked shout, turning the wheel too far in a panicked attempt to course-correct, skidding onto more ice. The whole car spun; the phone came loose of its holder and flew through the windscreen.

Glass cracked, spreading like a spiderweb across Neil's field of vision. He shouted again, wrestling with the wheel, before finding himself momentarily weightless.

Time slowed, and he was out of his seat, floating in the air; tiny triangles of glass hovered around him, his CDs loosed from the glovebox. Then the car struck the ground, rolling, shattering, crashing, groaning. Metal buckled, windows exploded, and Neil was thrown from one side of his seat to the other, the seatbelt barely holding on, biting into his throat. He struck the roof multiple times. The airbags sprang into life.

Everything hurt. The car continued to careen down the cliff-face. Cuts appeared on Neil's arms and face. Blood seeped into his white shirt, staining it red. A trail of discarded bodywork and shattered glass were left in the vehicle's dreadful wake.

Neil's head snapped forward, darkness enveloped his vision, and then all was still.

Vision returning, Neil saw a blanket of snow had entered through the now non-existent front window, covering the dashboard and swallowing most of his steering wheel. The heater was dead, and invisible ribbons of ice were reaching into the crumpled carcass of the car, sapping what little heat remained. His fingers, already assaulted by the earlier chill, gained no benefit from the dark blood that now stained them. Neil tried to flex his damaged digits, but doing so sent sharp pains shooting up his arms.

No. These were definitely not reasonable circumstances.

The blizzard continued to swirl around the battered remains of the vehicle, half-buried in a snow drift—this thick bank of snow had spared him from a particularly gruesome death. At this rate of snowfall, however, it wouldn't take long for the entire car to disappear beneath a frozen mound; Neil realised this with immediate alarm as, within seconds, the narrow view out of the driver-side door disappeared.

An image of a frostbitten body flashed through his mind, with icicles in his eyelashes and skin turned blue. Trapped in his seat within an icy tomb, the snow building up outside, would he suffocate first, or freeze?

His chest screamed; some small semblance of warmth returned to his fingers. Shaking the frightful picture from his mind, Neil fumbled with the seatbelt, struggling to get a grip on the switch. The belt itself rested against his neck, rubbing against a fresh cut every time Neil moved.

Unclipping himself, fingers aching, Neil could not stop himself from slipping forward and striking the steering wheel with his ribs. Air *whooshed* out of his lungs, followed by a pained cough. Pushing himself away from the wheel, his hand pressed on the horn. A weak beep barely made it through the snow, then died.

Well, shit . . .

Wrapping his wounded arms around the headrests for

leverage, Neil tried to drag himself into the back. Gripping anything proved difficult, for the cold had seeped into his bones, numbing his nerves, and there was little to push his feet off of. They simply sank into snow, socks made wet by the invading ice.

A stabbing pain, like a hundred knives piercing his spine, ran down his back; he was breathless in moments, but the pressing desire for escape gave him the strength required. A few muscle-tearing tugs later, and he was past the handbrake and into the back.

His head spun as he leant against the driver's seat, everything twisted in a slow-passing blur, like an impressionist painting. He took a slow breath, and everything righted itself again. He was, though, still stuck in the car, and the snow was beginning to cover up the remains of the back windows too.

Looking around the crumpled confines around him, Neil spotted his coat under the passenger seat. Tugging it free caused the car to shift, and his heart beat with a renewed intensity. The vehicle couldn't sink any further into the snow, surely? He decided it wasn't worth finding out; shrugging into the coat, knocking his arms against the roof in the process; Neil then hurriedly checked the pockets for anything that might aid in his plight.

To his fortune, and Deborah's credit, the pockets had been stuffed with a pair of woollen gloves and a matching hat. For the first time, Neil was thankful for his wife's obsessive worrying over weather forecasts.

Though touched by the encroaching cold, the garments he was now wrapped in succeeded in lessening the chill. The numbing touch of ice on his nerves faded, and moving his fingers was less painful within the soft confines of the gloves. Outside the car, however, the snow had gathered almost to the tops of the back windows, spilling onto the seats through the shattered frames. Grey light was quickly turning to black as the piling powder attempted to block out the light, and trap Neil inside.

He gathered his strength, took a deep breath, and then pushed himself off the driver's seat and toward the rearmost window. Scrambling like a first-time rock climber, his feet slipped against the leather of the backseats, arms complaining as he reached for the twisted frame of the boot door. Cold metal attempted to steal the heat from his hands. Snow and shards of glass fell around him, biting the cuts on his face, the wind doing all it could to push him back.

With a half-groan, half-shout, Neil hefted himself up and out of the car. It took all his remaining strength not to pitch face first into the mound of snow surrounding him, barely able to rest upon the cadaver of his automobile.

Gazing out into the whirl of windswept snow, he wondered just how far from the road he was. It wasn't a particularly tall cliff face—that much he was aware of from almost daily drives along it—but it would be impossible to climb his way back up. Even if the rocks were dry and the wind was still, Neil was no mountaineer.

Perhaps, then, his best option was to sit tight. It was icy cold out here, yes, but he had his hat and gloves. Perhaps he could siphon some fuel out of the car and set it alight for some warmth. He could see a silver lining already: he had been on the phone at the time of the crash, after all; surely Deborah would have called the authorities. People would be on their way to help him, so all he had to do was sit tight and wait.

Right?

The wind was biting, seeking entry into every fold of the coat, attempting to bypass Neil's attempts at remaining warm. Though the coat was, so far, succeeding in its defence, all the heat in his face was draining away. Cheeks went rosy, and his nose lit up. For now, though, it was tolerable, as long as he could keep the coat pulled tight. He tried to cover his face with the collar, but it wasn't quite high enough.

Unsheltered, the snow gathered around his shoulders and soaked into his trousers. After an assumed four minutes atop the crashed car Neil was beginning to notice ice crystals forming on his legs. A glance inside the vehicle showed it had almost filled with snow, much of it sluicing off the mound that surrounded him. Despite the gloves and hat, his nerves were beginning to numb again. Shivers did little to generate warmth, and every slight shuffling of his legs was like attempting to move a fallen tree.

I can't stay here. I'll freeze before anyone finds me, he told himself. Another voice inside his head, though, warned that if he left the snow might swallow his tracks. There was no escape from this storm, but at least he'd receive a proper burial if he stayed put.

It was hard to chase away the hopelessness inherent in that thought. Walking was hardly going to change his fate. Maybe doing so would keep the blood pumping a little longer, but eventually it would turn to ice in his veins. Yet again an image of a dreadful demise flashed in his mind; this time he was frozen in place, as though someone had pressed the pause button as he walked. A frozen statue, dusted with frost and snow.

He pulled the coat as tight as he could, warding off the more violent tremor that ran through his body. He couldn't feel his nose anymore, and feared the red may be turning to purple. Trying to flex his toes, he felt nothing within his shoes, though a subtle spark of pain shot up his shin.

A tear froze beneath his eye, pinching skin. He wiped it away. *Oh, Deborah . . . I'm sorry . . .*

His passing would break her heart. It had only been a month since they'd discussed finally trying for a baby, but work had gotten in the way, much as it had for the past six years. The biological clock was ticking, and they both knew it. If only Neil had made it home. He would have welcomed being snowed in to finally start working towards that dream.

He wiped away more icy droplets as they gathered on

his cheeks.

Come on, man. Fight through it for her. Stay alive.

As if in response to his gathering determination, the whirling wind renewed its assault, seeming to change direction so that all the snow carried upon its invisible waves was swept toward Neil's shivering, freezing form. He sputtered as flakes the size of stones struck his lips, trying to force their way inside his mouth. If the blizzard couldn't freeze his skin, it would freeze his organs from within.

Covering his mouth with his hands, Neil realised that the wool had been soaked through by partially melted snow. His breath was barely warm enough to make a difference, though he could at least feel the tingling in his skin now, and the snowflakes' assault had been blocked.

By protecting his face, however, he was no longer holding his coat quite so tight. The cold crept in through his collar, an unpleasant, skin-crawling caress worming its way over his skin. Cuts cried out; warm blood was drained of heat. An awful, spine-aching shiver ran through the entirety of Neil's body, a thick cloud of white vapour gathering before his red, purpling face.

His eyelids started to droop.

I could just fall asleep . . .

Neil knew he shouldn't, but his body was beginning to have its own ideas. It would conserve energy to keep him alive; he would be snow-dusted, encased in ice, and all his rescuers would have to do would be warm him back up.

A thin smile formed on Neil's face as his eyes closed. He forced them back open, but they didn't stay that way for long. His body began to shift, to roll, laying down upon the cold, crumpled metal of the car, cushioned by the snow.

Perhaps he would have fallen asleep there, and succumbed to a snowy death, had the buried vehicle's frame not proven too narrow. Instead, Neil rolled off the roof, dropping into the snow like a branch from a tree. The immediate freezing touch had the same effect on Neil as a bucket of water on a heavy sleeper.

Leaping to his feet, knees lost in the snow drift around him, Neil barely even registered the protestations of his muscles. He was more aware of the hammering of his heart, shocked into palpitation by the forceful awakening. Snow clung to his hat, gloves and coat, his face wet, with icy crystals already nipping his skin. Instantly he pulled the coat tight again, arms shaking as his newfound wakefulness reminded him of the intensity of the cold.

Shuddering breaths prevented words, though he wished he could shout out into the swirling snowstorm and damn it. Damn it for what he wasn't quite sure, but a vicious catalogue of curses were on the tip of his tongue.

I haven't succumbed to the cold yet, he told himself, drawing strength from this silent defiance. *I'm going to survive this. I just have to stay put and they'll find me.*

Where before the storm had punished him for his rush

of resolve, now it seemed impassive, ignoring his presence. Continuing to whirl around him, an indifferent, monochromatic blanket, this blizzard was now content to wait rather than attack. It no longer needed to sap the warmth from Neil's bones, nor was it necessary to plant ice in his organs.

The storm had played its part. Now it was something else's turn.

As Neil found the inner strength necessary to overcome the bone-aching, muscle-gripping, nerve-numbing cold, a rumbling roar echoed through the grey expanse around him. The origin was unclear, for it seemed to come from everywhere, a part of the very fabric of reality. Upon first hearing it, despite the bunching up of his shoulders, Neil simply assumed it was thunder, or perhaps a sheet of snow falling from the cliffs.

Then it came again, slightly different in tone, the echo enduring. There was a growl-like quality to that noise, suggestive of a roving predator more than meteorological phenomena. If Neil hadn't already been shivering, with the cold consuming him, then an unpleasant chill would have surely crawled up his spine. Instead his breath hitched, and he took a slow step backwards.

Snow crunched, not just under his feet but ahead of him, within the chaos of rushing ice. Neil remained still, but the crunching continued, getting louder with each apparent step. Something was getting closer; the bestial bellow sounded again, closer, louder, overcoming the wind's attempts to sweep it away.

Neil turned and ran.

A panted half-scream broke from his throat as he stomped through the snow, running like a child in deep water, away from whatever had been approaching him. There were no bears or wolves in the UK, he was certain, not even hidden away within the expansive fields and rolling hills that characterised Yorkshire.

But something was definitely coming after him. Something big.

Looking over his shoulder revealed nothing; it was like looking at an out-of-tune television set, snow rendering him almost blind. There were no shapes within the storm, no towering shadows or darting figures, only the constant falling of flakes carried on a hateful tempest. Neil's heartbeat hammered harder.

Huffing, spirals of frozen breath trailing behind him, he kept pumping his legs through the snow. It clung to him, pulling him back like a frozen thorn bush. The unseen predator bellowed behind him again, its shout swallowed by the whistle of the wind. Neil dared to hope he had put some distance between himself and it, but did not slow down. Not yet. It was still audible, and that meant it was still too close.

The forceful buffeting of the wind, and a dizzying chill in his ears, robbed him of all sense of direction. That he was headed away from the car he was certain, as he hadn't stumbled upon any of his own tracks yet, but there was no telling whether he was still anywhere close to the road. His muscles complained at the work they were being forced to undertake, his fearful focus fading.

Neil considered stopping. A growl pierced through the high-pitched shrilling of the blood-chilling wind, and he instantly pushed himself harder, despite the protestations of his limbs.

Assaulted by face-numbing, nose-biting cold, time lost all meaning. He had no idea how long he had been sat upon the car before that terrible rumble tore through the monochrome gloom, and he certainly did not know how long he had been running. The aching in his bones suggested a lengthy trek, but such sensations were deceitful at best. Neil knew the cold had drained his body of strength long before this panicked excursion into the icy void.

As though acknowledging this fact stole his last vestiges of energy, Neil pitched forward into the snow, landing face first. The flakes thrown up by his impact were immediately lost to the wild wind. Icy wetness soaked in through his gloves, biting into his fingertips and clawing up his arms. It was like sticking his limbs into a bucket full of ice cubes. Neil hissed against the pain.

His eyes insisted on closing again. He was laying down anyway; why shouldn't he sleep now? If whatever had come across him returned, wouldn't he rather be asleep when it ate him? He wouldn't feel anything. The cold would make sure his nerves were numb. Proving the point, the snow's touch crept further into his flesh. Neil was certain he could feel his bones tingling.

No ... I have to get back to Deborah ...

Pushing himself up, pain tore through Neil's petrified tendons. A tremble coursed through his body, all warmth sapped from his muscles. Tingling consumed his extremities, pins-and-needles in every inch of his being. He sobbed, then shouted, and tipped back so that he was kneeling on the ground. Snow clung to his face, his skin tight against his scalp. The hat had slipped up off his ears, and Neil hurried to pull it back down. He could almost hear Deborah's admonishments; *keep your ears warm,* that's what she'd say, her smile enough to chase away the cold.

He wiped the snow from his face before it could freeze his eyes open—or worse, closed. No mist gathered before him, and he couldn't help but wonder just how far his body temperature had fallen. How long until he succumbed to hypothermia? Fear of frostbite flashed through his mind, but he resisted the urge to look beneath his gloves. His fingers were still tingling, so they must have still been alive.

Taking a long, deep breath that chilled his lungs but woke his senses, Neil was about to stand when a familiar sound returned.

Crunching. Steady, heavy crunching as snow was crushed beneath approaching feet. Big feet making sinister, stomping steps. Steps getting closer, closer, closer ...

Neil had never enjoyed the rush of adrenaline. He hated rollercoasters, loathed practical jokes, and felt sick after any shock when driving. For the first time in his life, however, he was glad that it flooded his system now. All pain was driven from his mind with a red-hot poker, his muscles primed and ready to run.

More crunching, another barking bellow, and Neil was sprinting again. He swept what snow he could out of his path, breathless and cold but refusing to slow. Behind him the crunching got faster, but mercifully no louder, accompanied by a ghostly grumble that eerily reflected his own panicked breathing.

He did not look behind himself this time—he recalled the futility of doing so before—and instead put all his fear-fuelled energy into eluding the spectral stalker. His senses zeroed in on the weighty footsteps, noting that they faded with each crunch; the huffing and puffing disappeared with them.

A smile formed across Neil's frozen face as he realised that, for the second time now, he had evaded the mysterious predator lurking in the storm. Adrenaline carried him further, but as relief flowed through him, so too did the chemical fade away. Leaden lethargy returned to his legs, the racing of his heartbeat reflecting fatigue rather than fear. After a handful of heavier steps all he could hear was the rushing of the blood in his veins, overcoming even the relentless cries of the remorseless blizzard. He knew that to stop could allow the prowler in the storm to catch up again, but his body had expended the last of its energy, allowing him one final escape.

His stomach twisted as his legs gave out, forcing Neil to his knees. The thick cushion of snow softened his fall, nerves robbed of all sensation so that he almost felt as though he was floating, no longer touching anything. Though shivers wracked his body, the cold itself was distant now, little more than a tickle on his skin. Gulping in a great lungful of frigid air, Neil could almost imagine he was breathing in solid ice, yet he was grateful to still be breathing.

They must have found the car by now, he told himself. *Maybe they'll see my tracks. They can follow them and find me, hopefully before whatever that creature is does. I should just stay put and stay quiet. Stay put. Stay quiet.*

A cloudless yawn forced itself free of his breast, his ice-locked jaw grinding like a rusted hinge. Closing his mouth again proved more painful than opening it. Then, shuffling in the snow, every muscle falling asleep, Neil rolled over like an awkward, clumsy infant, and spread himself out as though he were about to make snow angels.

The sky was gunmetal grey, throwing ferocious flakes of snow at him; ice formed around his eyes, and when he blinked, they would not open. He should have panicked, but he had no energy left for panic. He wouldn't be there for long; the rescue team must be right behind him. They would have scared the beast of the blizzard away, and any second now they'd wrap him in blankets and lift him into a nice warm four-by-four.

Within an hour they'd have him rushed to hospital, no doubt with Deborah in tow. A faint smile cracked the frost on his face as he pictured her panicked tears, and heard her quivering voice berating him for making her worry so much.

'I told you to drive slowly, you idiot. You didn't have to rush.'

'Look on the bright side,' Neil would whisper back. 'You've got me all to yourself for a while.'

Once he was all warmed up, he'd wrap her into his arms, holding her close, more grateful than ever to feel her warmth against him. Under no circumstances would he be heading straight back to work, not after an accident like this; nothing mattered except being back with Deborah, in the warmth of their home, finally taking the time for themselves that had been forsaken for so long.

This would be one hell of a story to tell the kid, he considered. *Oh yes, I was lost in a snowstorm being chased by a huge, hungry monster!*

Crunching in the snow dragged him away from these comforting images; heavy, sinister and slow, like a cat stalking its prey. A vague rumbling drifted through the screeching storm, followed by a bellow, and an echoing growl. Neil's heart hammered in fear, then hesitated, and finally fell silent.

Let the beast come.

*

Three figures darted through the dancing swirl of windswept snow, wrapped in thick jackets and fluorescent yellow vests. Ice had encrusted their scarves and hats. One of the three rushed to Neil's side, skidding to his knees. He checked for breathing, dared to pull off his gloves, feeling for a pulse; it was useless.

His colleagues stood over Neil's still body and hung their heads. Their throats were hoarse from shouting through the raging wind, so they said no words. Instead, crystalline mist hovering before them, birthed of despairing sighs, they crouched down and aided in the retrieval of the purple-hued, ice-frosted body.

'The poor bastard,' one of the others muttered. 'God... his poor wife ... '

The wind stole the words away, preventing them from reaching her companions' ears.

Trudging back to their Land Rover, assaulted by icy shards of snow, the three would-be rescuers were grateful they would not be stuck out here for long. Blood-freezing wind whipped at their backs, whistling, keening, threatening to take them too.

A rumble rolled down from the sky, awakening an instinct in those three still-breathing souls that saw their pace increase, though the snow sought to hold them back. Caught in the roiling swirl, rushing toward the warmth and security of the waiting vehicle, hearts hammering, breath steaming, they were violently reminded that mother nature is rarely inclined toward mercy.

AUTHOR'S NOTE

When I saw the submission call for *Bitter Chills*, my first thought was 'Christmastime cosmic horror'. I played around with a few ideas, but none of them spoke to me. Only one or two of the dozen-or-so concepts I jotted down remain in my ideas list, and even those will require some in-depth rethinking. When the idea for "Snowblind" came to me, however, I knew it was a story I had to write. Something about rooting the story in a very real, very plausible kind of horror appealed to me.

It took a few drafts to get right, and I actually struggled with the story for a long time. In some ways, it was a very new experience for me. Pretty much every horror story I had written before this was heavily Lovecraftian—much like most of what I still write. *Snowblind* forced me to change how I approach horror, and to focus much more on the human experience and all the sensations connected with fear.

In the end, I was very happy with how it turned out—and even happier to discover it was being accepted for publication. The ending, especially, was something that took a long time to get right, and it was such a satisfying feeling when it clicked (in my eyes, at least, though of course I hope you like it too).

What is probably my favourite aspect of the story is that I managed to—or at least tried to—insert a touch of ambiguity. Whilst it is rooted in reality, I wanted to include that element of 'Is there something supernatural going on here?' And honestly, if you were to ask me, I would say 'I have absolutely no idea.'

Kyle J. Durrant

THE WILD HUNT
ROXIE VOORHEES

THE WILD HUNT

BY ROXIE VOORHEES

When the days have grown short and the winter chill has arrived, we visit a village in Norway. Geiranger is very small—only a few hundred residents live here—but one of the most important villages for trade throughout the area. A fjord of magnificent size and age walled within steep cliffs and filled with turquoise water. Home to killer whales, seals, and salmon, the fjord is the most impressive in the country and maybe even the world. Don't be fooled by its beauty, however; Geiranger is dangerous, and I am not referring to just the water.

We sweep through the trees and drift in a spiral of spinning snow to stop at a house. It is small, only one room, but the chimney billows smoke, and candles light its cavity. Like in most homes tonight, a little girl sits with her family in celebration of Mother's Night. The soft scent of oranges lingers near the doorway. They eat *borscht* and bread and drink mead then each little child is given a miniature *julekage*, finally joining around the hearth, and *bestemor* recites the Ásatrú prayer for Light's Return:

By Æsir and Alfar / And Dísir mighty
By Thunar's strong striking / And Freya's Hearth-fire
We seek the shining / Of Yule-morning's magic
Sunna we call you / Come forth from the night
Bear to us blessing / Of spring and then summer
Shine on our land / In our homes, in our hearts
Increase and bounty / Be ours and our kindred's
Rising light, welcome / we hail your returning

The littlest girl burrows deep in the hides on her bed and awaits her beloved *bestemor*. She tucks a lock of hair behind her ear, trying to stay on her best behaviour. '*Vær så snill*, please, tell me a story, *bestemor*,' her sweet little voice sings like bells chiming over the falling rain. 'Please, *bestemor*, or I won't be able to fall asleep. I'm much too excited.'

For tonight is the night before Yuletide, the Winter Solstice. Tomorrow will bring many chores and duties for each person to complete before the large gathering in the square. The old woman will take a jar of honey—the sweet, amber nectar from the gods—directly from the bees she keeps behind the home. Every year, after intimate celebrations with family, each villager will gather together in the square for a night of music and mead and merriment.

The little girl sits within her tiny dome of hope. Of course, *bestemor* cannot resist the innocence of this precious child. '*Lille venn*, I will. A story of Balder. Are you comfortable in your bed? There will be no leaving after I start this story.'

'Yes, *bestemor*, *Vær så snill*, please, tell me.' Her pale yellow curls bounce with excitement.

After a few quiet moments, the girl's grandmother makes her way to a small chair a few steps away. 'It was said,' she starts, with her voice low and soft, 'that the most beautiful of all of the Gods was Balder.' The old woman settles into her chair while the black forest cat, Skaði, whips her steps gracefully through its legs.

'You do know who Balder is, *barnebarn*?' She waits for the little girl to acknowledge her with a nod then continues, 'After he'd had some dark dreams, his mother, the goddess Frigg, vowed to scour the nine worlds and gather the promises of everything in nature, not to hurt him.

'Frigg, such a loving and caring mother, went to every tree, rock, beast, and on and on, collecting promises. When asked about mistletoe, the goddess proclaimed, "Mistletoe is far too young and weak to harm Balder," and so, Balder became nearly invincible and even more popular.' The old woman's eyes grow big as she uses her hands to animate her story.

'*Bestemor*, didn't the goddess worry mistletoe would grow bigger and stronger, like a child from a baby?' The little girl's concern is painted all over her face.

'*Jenta mi*, you are so smart. She may have forgotten

63

that, even though her brave, beautiful Balder could not be harmed by everything else, and young mistletoe had no intentions to harm the god, the evil in man could still twist things into his favour.'

'No, no, no. I don't like this story. It's sad.' The girl's plump lower lip sticks out and shudders. 'I want a happy story. *Vær så snill*, please, tell me a real story, *bestemor*. One that happened to you when you were little, like me.' Her golden hair falls around her face in ringlets as she bounces in excitement.

'*Ja, mitt skatt*, then it is bedtime. We have a big day tomorrow.' Streaks of grey scatter across the woman's cheeks as she sits back comfortably in the chair. 'This story takes place many, many moons ago. It has a girl and a boy and—'

'Is there kissing, *bestemor*? I don't like kissing.' The girl's disgust is apparent by the way she scrunches up her face when she sticks her tongue out.

Laughing, the grandmother responds, 'Well, maybe a little, but we can skip it if you want.'

'Please, *beste*,' the little girl's eyes sparkle in the candlelight.

'Very well,' the woman softly laughs and gently rocks herself while thinking of how to start the tale. 'Let's see. It was many, many dagmarks ago. Oh, yes. It was the winter solstice and I had gone to the market to find a new ribbon for my hair. I wanted to look the most beautiful, for my heart jumped at the thought of Rune, a boy from the other

64

side of the village, attending the gathering that night.'

'Did he?' Sitting upright in her furs, the little girl brushes a curl out of her eyes.

'Yes, *jenta mi*, he did. This is the story of Rune and the Wild Hunt.'

'The Wild Hunt? What is that, *bestemor*?' A little wrinkle furrows between her brows.

'Ah, yes, you haven't heard this tale yet.' The little girl has only experienced four full earth turns and there is much she has yet to learn. 'The Wild Hunt is an advance of Woden and the Yule Riders—ghostly warriors on their steeds in the winter sky. Woden always leads them, starting on *Samhain*, to collect all of the lost souls still on our world.'

'Where do they go?' her soft tinkle of a voice jingles out.

'Well, some go to Valhalla, and I assume some go to Hel. Many strange things happen as The Wild Hunt makes its way through the sky. And no matter what, do not find yourself outside after *miðnætti*. Do, and you will be swept up with the other lost souls and be gone forever.'

'Forever?' those sparkling eyes grow wider.

'Forever,' the old woman chokes on that, possibly choking back tears—unwanted memories attacking behind her eyes.

Not noticing, just like most children, the little girl lies back, hands propped behind her head. The candlelight flickering causes shadows to chase each other across the walls. The smell of sage drying overhead floods the room with a comfortable, safe scent.

'Rune lived on the far side of Geiranger, over the hill and a winding trail down. His father worked with mine, building ships down by the fjord. His mother often brought his siblings and him to the village square at midday. His sister was my age, he, a little older.'

She stops for a few breaths; brows furrow, lips tighten. 'I knew Rune for many years before that Yuletide. I had grown to love him and he loved me.' A timid smile peeks out for just a heart's beat. 'He told me so that night.'

'But *bestemor*, *bestefar's* name isn't Rune, it's Erik. He told me so when I asked why Onkel Anders was calling him that at supper.' This little girl was far too smart for courtesy's sake.

'No, *jenta mi*, I loved Rune before I did *bestefar*. May I continue?'

The child presses her lips firmly together in response.

'Once we returned home, Mor Astrid was very busy all day, and I had tried to sneak away back to the square to catch a glimpse of Rune before the gathering, but she kept her eye close on me.' A lighthearted chuckle leaves the woman's lips in remembrance.

'When I arrived, I began to search every face I could for the eyes of my future *mann* while still watching after my younger sister. Mor took her honey jar for offering, just like I do. She was looking for our village healer, while I looked for Rune.'

'Two sparkling orbs shone the colour of the North Sea in Spring. Sapphire spheres speared through me to my *sjel*. I knew, looking at him, that I wanted nothing more than to be with him for the rest of my days. Loyal, Honest, Trustworthy. He would be them all. And then some.'

Quiet tears begin to make streams down the woman's cheeks. There is the ever-so-slightest of quivers in her bottom lip, but no stranger to heartache, she continues her story.

'After Mor returned from the healer's tent, I sprinted away toward him without even a word. The smile on my face must have made me look rather foolish, but I didn't mind, not one bit. When I reached him, he grabbed my hand and led me behind the bakery hut.

'You have yet to live long enough to understand storms, *jenta mi*. When you are old like me, you can sense them far away from the scent. It smells of fresh earth buzzing like bees with excitement. You can sense a slight humming in the air, bouncing off your skin, if you are quiet and stay still enough to feel it.

'At Yule, we know any storm on the horizon is The Wild Hunt making its way through the sky. I was not the only villager that sensed the storm approaching, as everyone began to pick up their pace to finish the festival in enough time for them all to get home safely before midnight. Our Jarl was very superstitious and would never allow anyone to be out on that night.'

A sly smirk peeks out of one side of the old woman's

mouth. I know that Jarl, and he was right.

'Mor called me from the front of the bakery. I froze, so scared she would find me with Rune, but he hid in the shadow, whispering 'I'll wait for you', while I ran out to meet her. She needed help with my sisters while she helped Far with the lighting ceremony. I obeyed and decided to walk them down to the front of the area marked for the burning of the Yule Log.

'This log was not just a large branch like ours, *jenta mi*, no, it was an entire white oak bare of leaves, on its side, mourning deep roots and sunshine. This log would burn the full twelve days of Yule. We sat on the large rocks marking the barrier for the fire, while Mor spread the ashes from last year's log onto the trunk of the tree.'

Moments after she had left the embrace of young Rune, Herre Berg came right by him and requested his assistance with carrying goods home.

'Shouldn't you hurry, boy? It's almost midnight and you have far to ride yet,' Herre Berg told him.

Being an honourable young lad, Rune obliged, 'I have some time yet,' leaving the place he'd told the love of his life he would wait for her.

Nothing could possibly go wrong.

*

'It couldn't have been long since I'd left Rune, but he was not behind the bakery hut, where I'd left him. I began to search all over the square, hoping he'd walked down to see the burning. However, I couldn't find him anywhere. Shortly after, my mother and father called to me, beckoning me to come in order to prepare ourselves to leave.'

And in true serendipitous form, Rune returned to the bakery just mere moments after his love had left with her family. He searched the nearby huts but found no sign of her. He struggled visibly, wanting to find her but also needing to leave to get home before midnight.

'Superstition! It isn't real, Rune,' he chastised himself.

Precious moments were wasted while each searched for the other, impossibly missing one another over and over again. Alas, the young lad spotted her crimson locks, plaited in swooping waves. She turned to spot his serious, nautical gaze locked on her.

'I saw him. His dark, sea-blue eyes peered through me again. I felt my heart skip beats. I was scared but happy all at once. That was when I knew I loved him.'

Through a yawn, the little girl manages to get out, 'Loved him?'

'Yes, *lille venn*, very much so. Now off to bed, you are

rightly tired and have much to do tomorrow.' The old woman begins to stand.

'No, no. Please, *bestemor*, please finish the story. I am not tired yet.'

'Ah, a bit more, then sleep.' She settles herself again and picks up where she left off. 'I was going to skip the kissing part, but that is where I stopped. Rune held me in his arms and would not move his lips from mine. Moments went by and I grew afraid that midnight was coming far too quickly. I pulled myself away and managed to tell him to go, it was so late.'

'"I love you," he said to me, and kissed me one last time.' The woman brings her withered fingertips to her lips, taking a moment with the memory. 'He then ran as fast as he could to his horse, which was tied by the poultry house.'

'Oh, *bestemor*, I hope he makes it.' The little girl looks very concerned.

'Thick, fluffy flakes of snow began to fall, creating a colourless shroud over the square. People quickened their steps and father insisted we leave at once. I was very scared that if I didn't watch Rune ride away, he wouldn't make it home, but Far wouldn't ever have allowed it.'

'With heavy steps, I returned to my family and accompanied them to our home, here, where we drank Wassail and gathered by the fire. When our excitement faded and we settled to bed, a rumble of terrible thunder roared through the house. I laid in my bed, petrified, worried Rune would be caught in the storm, or worse.'

A soft whistle of breath forces itself between the little girl's lips and she sleeps, peacefully, impervious to the fate of Rune, which the old woman would have likely made up to spare the poor child the ugliness of heartbreak. That sound is the cue for the woman to gather herself and slip to the dreamland that makes her safe. *Safer*, not safe. Rune is in her dreams. She thinks of him every single day. Days with her loving husband make it easier, but that pain is always hiding under the thin veil she uses to cover the crack in her heart.

As she walks toward her sleeping area she mutters in a whisper to herself what really happened, what she found the next morning. 'I never saw him again after that.'

Large, warm tears drop like falling stars down the curves of the old woman's cheeks. She clutches at her chest with both hands, as if holding the pieces of her heart together.

The storm outside now is much like the one of that Yule night, bringing chaos and destruction along its path like a moving battlefield.

Heavy shavings of ice seemed to fall sideways as Rune attempted to make it up the large hill on the far side of Geiranger. Over the hill and through the woods, he would find his family's humble home tucked to the north, his parents likely worried about him.

The thick, threadbare, woollen cape his mother had given him after his father got a new one was not working. Large pelts of snow landed on the back of his neck, melting and creating rivers of icy remains, sending chills down his spine in a quite literal fashion. He wrapped it as best he could while still holding onto the horse's reins, but the wind was ruining any hope of that.

The horse, Gunnar, was a strong steed and his father's and he was certain if he didn't return the horse—rightly so—his father may drown him. 'Good boy Gunnar, fresh hay when we get home. I'll even give you the fur from my own bed, just get us home.' The boy looked anxious, like maybe he was regretting looking for his love for so long.

Just then his fingers let go of the cape, sending it whipping backward with a sharp *crack*. He brought them to his lips, to the space hers once were, the space he wanted them to be again. He licked his lips as if searching for the taste of her lingering behind.

Gunnar was as steady and sure-footed as any fjord horse, but the snow blanketed the path into a fluffy feather bed and he tripped in a hole filled deep with it. The horse shrieked in agony and stumbled a few steps. Rune patted his neck and silently said a prayer to Sleipnir, relieved that the horse hadn't fallen.

At last, they reached the top of the hill. Normally, Rune would look back down at the fjord and all the lights, but not tonight; tonight he had no time to waste. If he had looked back; however, he would have seen the storm slithering its way up the fjord toward the port.

In front of him was the wood he needed to pass to get home. 'Almost there boy,' Rune encouraged Gunnar to go faster. But the woods were pitchy. There was no light except the torch he held that threatened to fizzle out at any breath. The smell of damp earth and sweat punctuated his thoughts as he smiled again; thinking of her taste on his lips made his heart warm his body.

The horse was spooked when wolves howled at the full moon. They smelled his fear and began to follow. As they closed in, Gunnar reared back, making Rune fall off the pack saddle. His foot became entangled in the reins of the fjord horse. Dangerously close to being stepped on, Rune freed a knife from his belt and cut the reins. He fell with force, onto his back between two large trees. The horse ran off.

'Coward.'

Swiping at the snow stuck to his backside, Rune looked up at the moon just as a parade of ghostly men on horses rode across the sky.

I remember *Fimbulwinter*, the awful winter, told as a cautionary bedtime story to little children—when snow falls in every direction, the land is thick with frost, and sharp winds slice like blades. Three winters like this will go by, with no summer in between, such as the winter to come. Then *Ragnarok* will be upon us.

This story was heavy in Rune's heart as he looked around to soak in his surroundings—skeletons of trees, gnarled and crooked, whipping in a dance of bad omens. The torch he carried had fizzled out with his tumble and now only by the permission of Mani did the full moon light the snow a soft yellow. Large flakes sparkled the night air like bright stars falling from the sky. Over his left shoulder, Rune heard the flat thud of something landing in the snow, beyond the copse of trees to the North. Taking a gulp, he began to run in the opposite direction, hoping it was the way home.

Tree branches, naked of their summer coat, slapped Rune across the arm and whipped at his face in his abandon. His only goal was to reach the safety of his home before whatever he'd heard in those trees found him. The smell of wood-smoke tickled his nose, reassuring him that he was going in the right direction. The small home sat in a clearing on the other side of these trees—if he could just get out of them in one piece.

The burning ache in Rune's legs couldn't be ignored any longer and he slowed down and stopped for a short break to catch his breath. Heart pounding, making his eyeballs vibrate, and hands shake, he risked a look behind him. The shadows had gathered into large shapes with glowing red eyes.

The leader locked eyes with Rune and picked up his pace. The storm rolled in thunder behind them with evidence that a magical force was at work here.

The snow piled like stones building a wall, causing Rune to weave through patches of particularly deep accumulation. Fallen branches lay in his path; the weight of the heavy downfall had proved too much for their weakened limbs in the stinging wind. The wood-smoke grew stronger yet, and Rune smiled, sure he would make it home. A branch as thick as his thumb slammed into the bridge of his nose as he slid down a slick patch of the path and caused warm, salty blood to flow out of his nose and fill his mouth. He didn't stop.

Too close by to be comfortable, wolves howled, indicating they had joined in on the hunt. Rune weaved between trees, avoided the rocks and large roots, and made a straight line. His vision was impaired by the swelling taking over between his eyes; his nose was definitely broken. Fingertips frozen and numb, he brought them to the sore spot and quickly removed them with a wince. He could now see the smoke billowing out of the chimney from the top of his home.

A young man's agility was no match for the smooth surface of ice formed on the top of the packed snow. Rune had barely blinked his eyes when the ground below him disappeared and sent him into a freefall down the mountain. The mountain wasn't just a slope; it led straight down. He fell for so long, he was unsure how far it was, landing in a fluffy bed of powder snow—likely what saved his life.

Opening and closing his eyes with the pulsing beat of

his heart, Rune rolled to an upright seated position to take stock of his environment. His right arm was bent awkwardly and throbbed with such animosity, he may as well have cut it off. Unable to determine exactly where he was, he stared at the sky and searched for the brightest star indicating North.

Finding the star to his right, he turned to the left—his home should not be far in that direction. Taking a few steps, darkness began to creep around the bones of trees on the edge of Rune's vision. Walking faster through the deep snow, he hesitated for just a breath, wanting to see what was behind him, but just like his horse, he was a coward and continued forward. Large dark clouds slithered across the sky blocking the stars and finally the moon.

And he stood there thinking of her when it all went pitch.

Ever the loyal companion, the moon broke free of its clouded prison, giving the icy blue of the vicinity a soft, warm glow. Wolves growled behind Rune's head; he could not move to see just how close they were, but it didn't matter. They were patiently waiting for the scraps. Held down by the shadowy hands of Viking warriors he did not recognize, Rune mumbled under his breath about the woman he loved. 'Her curls of red vivid as fresh blood in the morning snow. She smells of pomegranates and earth.

Her kiss is the sweetest honey I have ever tasted. And I will never taste again.' Drifting in and out now, Rune was no longer afraid, only sad.

Safe and warm in her bed, Rune's love also thought of his kiss on her lips. The salty warmth of his memory lingered as she thought of all the kisses she would give him in the future. Outside the thunder roared, as Thor cracked his hammer against the clouds, shaking their home and everything in it. Letting out a quiet sigh of relief she laid prone, eyes locked above, as the rhythmic pelting of frozen snow dropping on the roof and whistling shriek of the wind imitated an argument outside that she could barely hear, so she listened more intently. Wind, as stubborn as a horse, passed under the door and caused the single candle lit to quaver underneath her loft. 'Please Freya, let Rune be home safe,' the girl murmured as she drifted to sleep.

The stench of rotting meat insulted the nostrils of the boy as he lay still—only a single freezing tear able to still move. *Draugr* had left their graves to assist Woden on his quest and many had gathered around the area Rune lay. One came forward and the sapphire glint off its obsidian bone sparkled in the moonlight, allowing him the distraction needed while it tugged at his innards and removed pieces to take back to the others, a mouthful smeared over the jagged pieces of black ice it used as teeth.

To the left, two large blackbirds flew in circles, finally landing on the gnarled broken pieces of an ash tree, laying on its side. Each cawed in Rune's direction as they settled their long dark feathers by shaking and rustling. The birds' landing caused a commotion amongst the shadows as they mutably held a conversation. Rune was not allowed permission to partake. His body still numb but noticeably empty, he was reluctant to find Woden standing over him, reaching into his body and touching his heart with a ghostly hand before pulling out Rune's soul.

Placing the soul in a satchel at his hip, Woden gathered Rune in one arm and tossed him over his shoulder. Rope tied around the boy's hands, he was hung off the back of Sleipnir along with the satchel, as Woden gathered the other Riders and the *draugr* fell back away into the darkened forest—to their graves until the next Wild Hunt. The snow no longer prickled his skin when each flake landed in a deathly reminder of his failure. He failed his *mor* and *far*, he'd failed *hans kjærlighet*, and he'd failed himself.

Rune had never been the strongest boy or the smart boy or the boy with the blade skills of a powerful warrior. All Rune had been able to practice and perfect into a skill fit for the most generous of Valkyries—the pure and certain love he felt for her.

Slipping one hand from the ropes, Rune snuck it into the satchel of the man who had cut him open like a deer. Without as much as a breath, he clutched the soul to his chest and ran back into the trees where he could hide while the others mounted their ghostly steeds and took flight into the pitch sky.

He sat in the snow, no longer cold, and waited for her to come.

Riding your father's horse through the skittering snow in the darkness was not your best idea and it will likely get you killed. Did you hear that? A wolf. Perfect. You are going to die. You are stupid and you are going to die.

'Quiet,' the old woman says in her sleep.

The storm had finally stopped blanketing our small village and now it was time to find Rune and tell him I loved him. Our fathers could set up our marriage soon, there was no reason to wait for Spring.

What was that smell? It smelled like an old, slaughtered goat that has sat in the sun and gone bad. How could it go bad in this cold?

Stopping, I saw what I'd feared the most in front of me, blinking. I wanted to think this was a dream, but sadly, this is a memory. The red splash caught her eye first and she couldn't stop looking at it. I'm not sure how she didn't notice the rest of the entrails sprawled out in a crude painting, still steaming with my body's heat. My horse was grazing nearby, a path of snow already melted and exposing a brilliant shock of green to the scenery.

'But I was there, waiting for you. I have followed you since and have loved you the same.' I step out from behind the trees to where she stands. 'I watched you age and grow and have a family. And I have loved you the same.'

'I have loved you every day since,' tears fill her eyes as she turns to me. 'But how can you be here; now?'

'This is the moment both of our hearts combined in pure love. I was here, and you there, and although you never knew, we were bound by that love, and still are. Freya offered me this gift the night Wodon stole my soul,' I held out the bright blue light of my soul in my hand for her to see. 'As long as I hold it, I can stay on earth, stay with you, but now it belongs to Freya, as does yours, and she will keep us together for the rest of eternity.'

With nothing left to say, I kiss her, my fair *rettferdig jomfru*, with carefree abandon. I stop only to smile at her and absorb the look on her face into my memory, *'Jeg elsker deg.'*

She says nothing; her smile shines like the first sunray on the darkest day.

*

Woken by the sound of melted snow outside, dripping in melodic bars of icy euphoria, the little girl quickly unwraps herself and races to her beloved *beste's* bed to wake her. 'It's Yule, *bestemor*, wake up.'

Shaking her sweet *bestemor* does nothing to stir her; neither does calling her name, or even pinching her nose. Concerned, the young girl leaves to get her mother. When they return together, the young girl's mother falls to her knees—burning hot tears crashing down her cheeks.

'Look, mama, she's smiling.'

AUTHOR'S NOTE

Tucked in a mighty fjord, Geiranger is the home to this tale. I picked Norway in particular for its geographical location of swollen waves and algid winters. In 1934, a mountain collapse caused a massive tsunami 60m high in nearby Tafjord, destroying it and neighbouring communities. Hollywood made a disaster movie in 2015, *The Wave,* depicting a future threat to the village of Geiranger. I mean, could there be a better place for an anthology titled *Bitter Chills*? Probably, but I am going to focus on the positive here.

So, why The Wild Hunt?

As I was gathering my holiday reading list, I noticed a pattern; every single one had to do with Christmas. Now, I have nothing against Christmas, but I am not a person that believes in celebrating holy or religious holidays of a religion I am not a part of (kind of blasphemous in my view). I do; however, celebrate pagan traditions of my Heathen ancestors, the biggest being Yule.

For the last two decades, I have gathered a Yule tree, complete with Norse decorations, a Yule log—although it's usually a fake because burning a log for twelve nights isn't really doable in modern times—and crafted a dinner of venison. On Mother's Night, my children all gathered around my mother in brand new PJs and she read them a story. This tradition has slightly faded out as they have become adults and I wanted to honour it here.

What is the Wild Hunt?

The Wild Hunt is a Norse legend. It begins on Samhain (Halloween) and lasts until the winter solstice. Think of it as a presession of ghosts, led by Odin, that ride ghostly horses through the sky around the world, gathering all of the lost souls on Earth. How intimidating would that be? As if eight huge Viking warrior ghosts weren't enough, they attract wolves and *draugr* and other creatures of the night. Don't fear, The Wild Hunt is avoidable; stay indoors after midnight on the solstice and whatever you do, do not make eye contact with the procession.

Apparently Rune forgot that bit.

Roxie Voorhees

GLOSSARY
NORWEIGAN TERMS USED IN
'THE WILD HUNT'

Æsir [awe-seer]
The Æsir are the gods of the principal pantheon in Norse religion. They include Odin, Frigg, Höðr, Thor, and Balder.

Alfar [all-far]
A term heavily influenced and altered over time, but which here refers to elves.

Ásatrú [os-saw-true]
Religion meaning Æsir belief, commonly called Heathenry.

Balder
God of Light, Son of Odin and Frigg.

Barnebarn [barn-nah-barn]
Norwegian for *grandchild*.

Beste [best-ah]
Shortened version of *bestemor*, Norwegian for *best*.

Bestefar [best-ah-far]
Norwegian for *grandfather*.

Bestemor [bes-ta-mor]
Norwegian for grandmother, *Beste* meaning *best*, and *mor* meaning *mother*.

Dagmarks
Scandinavian measurement of time.

Dísir [dee-sir]
Female spirits including Valkyries.

Far
Norwegian for *father*.

Freya [frey-ah]
Goddess of Fertility.

Frigg
Goddess of Marriage, Queen of Asgard, highest of goddesses.

Fimbulwinter [fem-bull-veen-ter]
Means Great Winter, immediately preludes Ragnarok.

Fjord [fee-yourd]
A long, narrow inlet with steep sides or cliffs, created by a glacier.

Hans kjærlighet [hons shaw-lee-het]
Norwegian for *his love*.

Hel
Goddess of the Dead.

Herre [hair-rah]
Norwegian for *master.*

Jarl [e-yarl]
A Norse chief.

Jeg elsker deg [yaeye elle-sker die]
Norwegian for *I love you.*

Jenta mi [yen-tah me]
Norwegian for *my girl.*

Julekage [yoo-lay-key-yah]
Norwegian Christmas bread.

Lille venn [lil-lay vin]
Norwegian for *little darling.*

Mani
In Norse, the moon personified.

Mann [man]
Norwegian for *husband.*

Mitt skatt [Meet ska]
Norwegian for *my treasure.*

Miðnætti [min-nigh-tea]
Icelandic for midnight.

Mor [more]
Norwegian for *mother.*

Onkel [own-kell]
Norwegian for *uncle.*

Rettferdig jomfru [rett-fir-di yom-froo]
Norwegian for *fair maiden.*

Samhain [sow-ven]
The night the veil between the living and the dead is thinnest; signifies the start of winter.

Skaði [Sky]
Goddess of Winter.

Sjel [shell]
Norwegian for *soul.*

Sleipnir [s-lie-p-near]
An eight-legged horse ridden by Odin; lore says Loki gave birth to Sleipnir.

Sunna [soon-nah]
Norse Goddess of the Sun.

Thunar [thoo-nar]
Old Saxon name for God of Thunder.

Vær så snill [vash saw sneel]
Norwegian for *please.*

Valhalla [val-hall-ah]
Majestic hall located in Asgard.

Valkyrie [val-care-rhea]
Norse mythology; female figures that chose the slain warriors for Valhalla.

Wassail [vos-uhl]
Yuletide drink of mulled cider with spices.

The Wild Hunt
Folklore of northern European cultures: a group of ghostly men on horse,s usually led by Odin and said to be a bad omen if witnessed in the sky.

Woden
Alternate spelling of Odin, chief Norse God.

Yule
A festival celebrated historically by Germanic cultures dated before the celebration of Christmas.

Yule log
Traditionally a white oak log burned in the hearth for the duration of Yuletide, ashes are kept and spread on the next year's log.

Yule Riders
Ghostly warriors upon horses traveling through the sky to capture lost souls.

Yuletide
Synonymous with Christmas season, the twelve nights some Germanic cultures celebrate Yule.

THE COLD, THE GRIEF

SPENCER HAMILTON

THE COLD, THE GRIEF
BY SPENCER HAMILTON

I don't wanna go, Daddy. It's so cold over there.

Dustin woke screaming his son's name.

Consciousness came to him in quick, frigid bites. He was in the tent. And his son was gone. His son had been gone for days now. And he was never coming back.

Dustin sat up, extricating himself from the sleeping bag with stiff limbs. Already his entire body was shaking, whether from the cold or from the black depths of grief he did not know. That was the first thing he learned about the world without his boy. Everything was the same. Life was an indiscernible landscape on the horizon, and you'll never reach it no matter how hard you push through the cold and despair, which were just as indistinguishable from one another as that far horizon of snow and sky.

He clapped his hands together as he shrugged his body into more layers of clothing. He boiled water for coffee. He forced himself to chew and swallow some jerky and dried fruits.

He stepped out of the tent and promptly threw up his breakfast.

As he straightened up and tried and failed to see the exact line of the distant white horizon, he spit the bitter bile and said, his breath billowing ghosts into the air:

'What the hell are you doing out here, Dust?'

Dustin was ice fishing.

That was all he knew—and he knew even less about *how* to ice fish. But his dad's old cabin had been the only place he could think of after the funeral. The only place he could disappear to that people would nod and say, 'Take your time. Grieve at the cabin, yes, that sounds perfect. Just what your boy would have wanted.'

They hadn't a clue what his son would have wanted— all those blank faces from the funeral, none of them had known the boy, known him like his father had known him.

That's why you really *came to the cabin, Dust,* a voice whispered in his head. *Your boy begged you to bring him here, but you never did, and now the guilt is killing you like the leukaemia killed him.*

He ignored the voice. He ignored his shaking hands. His boots crunched across the lake and he came to rest on an upside-down bucket, his fishing rod lying beside it.

So he'd come to the cabin, the very night after burying his boy six feet underground. The boy's mother screamed at him as he left, but he couldn't scream back. Not anymore. None of that mattered now. For some reason he couldn't place, all that mattered was getting to the cabin. And then all that had mattered was getting drunk on his dad's old whiskey. And *then* all that had mattered was breaking every single framed picture in the damned place—his boy, mercifully, in none of them—and getting out of there.

He supposed it was a good thing he hadn't gotten back into his truck. Dustin had always despised people who drove drunk—or, to put a name to it, despised his father. He'd kill himself before he became like his father. It's why he'd never come to his dad's cabin before now, why he never brought his son here no matter how much he begged. And now he'd never bring him here. Seven years old and all his dreams snuffed out forever.

Instead, Dustin found himself standing outside his dad's old shed. He found himself drunkenly ripping the rotted door from its hinges and rampaging through the shed's innards. He didn't stop until he came to the old diesel auger. Something about that metal rod, with the scything swirl of blade along its length, calmed him. And with it, a memory:

Daddy, Grampa told me about the ice fishing. I wanna see!

He'd given his son a startled look, almost fearful. His own father had passed away years before, a heart attack. His boy never got a chance to know his grampa, even if Dustin would have let him.

'Grampa ... told you?' he'd asked, his throat dry, aching for a drink. 'What do you mean, buddy?'

But the kid wouldn't relent on the ice fishing: he

wanted to learn. Dustin had tried to explain that it would be boring, that he didn't even know how himself, but his son didn't care—

And now he was dead and gone. Seven years old and his father had never taken him fishing.

So a drunken Dusty, in the middle of the blackest winter night, had piled all of his dad's old gear in a sled—jigging rod, tackle, auger, ice saw, tent, a whole tangled mess of odds and ends—and gone careening off into the dark, in the general direction of what his dad had called the "best waters for fish in all of Maine".

You never took your boy fishing.

'Shut up,' he told the voice.

Sitting on the bucket, he took the fishing rod and fed its line down through the hole between his boots, a slender throat dipping into the depths of the lake. He almost chuckled—he was impressed with his drunk self of the previous night, cutting a hole into the ice like this. Surprised he didn't chop off a hand and bleed out in the snow.

Surprised . . . or disappointed?

Dustin sat there for hours, trying to ignore the thoughts in his head. His thoughts were a constant kaleidoscope of his son and wife and father and hospitals and divorce hearings and funerals and, before that, all the things they did together but would never do again.

You never took your boy fishing.

He'd tried drowning out that damn voice last night, but

it didn't take.

Dammit. He forgot the whiskey.

Dustin was sobering up and he didn't like it. At least he had this hangover to stop the kaleidoscope of memories. At least he had the cold to numb him. His breath to keep him company. The never-ending horizon to watch over him.

What he was doing was pointless. Stupid. He hadn't caught a single damn thing after hours of sitting here, and he wasn't going to if he sat here till Hell froze over. But for some reason he couldn't bring himself to pack up and admit defeat.

He barely recalled enough from his childhood to get the fishing rod working, barely remembered enough to know to put bait at the end. Some contraption sat uselessly to the side, discarded out of frustration; he was pretty sure it was meant to be set up over the hole so it could cradle the fishing rod. It crouched now like some Mesozoic insect dredged up from the ice and cast aside.

But whatever. He needed to hold on to something anyway.

The hours passed in monotonous, monochromatic white. The lake stretched as far as he could see in every direction, his tent the only thing out here. Every few hours he replaced the jig just to have something to do, lest his hands freeze.

Thoughts of his father crept up on him. Dustin's father spent so much of his time at this stupid cabin. Had he sat in this exact spot, in the middle of the lake, on this exact bucket? Also cradling a nasty hangover, no doubt.

His father had always tried to lure him out here, to teach him. Years later, his own son begged him to take him out here, to teach *him*. And the whole time, what did he do?

Said *no*.

The worst part? He remembered those first hospital visits, after the diagnosis, seeing his son in the hospital bed, just skin and bones, and hearing that small voice in the back corner of his mind, whispering, *Well . . . at least you don't have to say no anymore.*

'You're a piece of shit, you know that?' he muttered out loud, dragon smoke pouring from his mouth.

But he was here now. And he'd catch a fish for his son if it was the last thing he did.

Maybe *that* was why he was here. A part of Dustin—the drunk part—had thought this would be a good spot to kill himself. His own father had died in his favourite armchair back at the cabin, and his boy had begged him to come here to fish before *he* died, so it made a kind of sense.

But the more he sat out here thinking on things, the more he decided that would be a slap in the face to his son. Commit suicide, in the exact place he refused to take his boy? That would make him a coward—would make his wife right about him. And if he found his boy on the other

96

side, waiting for him? Could he stand the look of sad disappointment?

So . . . no. He was here to make amends.

He was here to teach his boy how to ice fish.

A full day, come and gone. Not one fish.

Dustin's teeth chattered. His body shook. He no longer felt his legs.

But still he sat there. He'd get his boy a damn fish.

He remembered the worst day of his life so clearly it was almost as if he were still living it. A perpetual, purgatorial time loop. Never ending, never relenting, a horizon he'd never reach but always trudge towards.

It was the day they both died—his boy, there on the hospital bed, and Dustin, wishing he could go with him wherever he went in death. But it was behind a horizon he couldn't reach. He was a coward either way.

These were the sorts of thoughts that had been chasing him for months as he sat by the hospital bed, trying to ignore the voice. He stood watch as his boy's hand became smaller, frailer, colder in his own.

On the day, Dustin dozed. He woke with a start, certain beyond a shadow of a doubt that he was at his father's old cabin, sitting in the same armchair where they'd found his dad's corpse. He was certain of this, and certain that this same corpse, all bloated and seeping lake water, was standing over him, grinning down at him with an almost lecherous leer.

How's 'bout I teach you how to handle a fishing rod, Dusty?

And then, spewing whiskey-choked laughter into his face, his father slapped a gutted fish into his hand. It was the cold, slimy feel of the thing that woke him.

He jerked awake in his chair, itchy with sweat.

No. Not the cabin. The hospital room. Always the hospital room.

He remembered the dead fish in his hand, but when he looked it was just another, smaller hand, skeletal and cold as ice. His eyes rolled slowly up the hospital bed, a moan rising from his gut at what he might see.

'What if I fall in, Daddy?'

Intense relief burned his eyes. His boy was still alive. For now.

The question registered as he woke fully. 'Fall in where, buddy?'

'When you take me fishing. What if I fall in the water? My legs don't work too good anymore . . .'

It took another moment for him to realize what his boy meant. His heart sank.

The fishing again.

'I'll catch you, son,' he whispered, trying for a smile but crying instead. 'I'll always catch you.' He looked away—he hated himself for it, but more and more he'd found he lacked the courage to look directly at his boy as he withered away to nothing.

'But what if something pulls me down?'

The question froze the blood in his veins. His throat constricted, but he managed to choke out one last promise: 'I'll pull you out, of course.'

His boy didn't seem to hear him. Those ocean-blue eyes swam, sunken in their sockets, then latched on to their father's, suddenly panicked. His hand, weak like the rest of him, remained limp, a dead fish in Dustin's grasp.

'I don't wanna go, Daddy. It's so cold over there.'

As the last of the light bled from the sky, making its final kaleidoscopic tilt from white to black, Dustin felt a tug.

'Sh-sh-shit!'

He curled his numb fingers around the rod tighter. Sat up straighter.

What was he supposed to do now? Pull up?

He thought of his son's words—*Grampa told me about ice fishing*—and how they had plucked a shiver up his spine. Dustin's old man had died when his son was just a baby, and yet . . . Dustin saw his father again, standing over him, bloated with lake water, slapping the dead fish in his hand . . . maybe he *had* told his grandson about the greatest ice fishing spot in Maine.

'If you're there,' he said now, the fishing line still tugging in the dark, 'guide my hand, old man. Help me. Put all our bullshit aside. You're a bastard and I'm a son of a bitch, doesn't matter. Water under the bridge. But here. Now. Let's do this . . . for him.'

He held his breath, listening for an answer. His father's rusty chuckle, the voice in his head—the voice of God Himself—something. Anything.

Nothing.

Tink.

There, right there, half a foot below the surface: a sharp knock against the ice.

Warmth spread through Dustin's body. Whatever was down there, it was *big*.

'Hole's not big enough,' he breathed. 'Dammit, hold on!'

He fell to his knees and wrestled the fishing rod into the discarded cradling contraption. It wasn't properly set up, but it would have to do—all he needed was a minute, one minute to take the ice saw, the one he'd found with the auger and thrown in the sled with the rest of it, and hack away some of the ice.

His heart slammed against his chest as he thrust the saw into the slushy ice beside the hole. He made quick work of it, unaware of the smile that broke onto his face, like sunlight through storm clouds, for the first time since the leukaemia diagnosis.

Dustin dropped to his knees again, the saw clattering away, and snatched the rod before it could be tugged into the newly widened hole in the ice.

'Okay, Dad,' he muttered, heaving with exertion. 'What

next?'

But there was no answer, of course. Not from his dad, or from the voice in his head.

There was, however, an answer from beneath the ice.

Tink.

'No way,' Dustin breathed. '*Still* too big?'

But just as he was about to drop the pole again and return to hacking away with the saw, he caught sight of something in the water. Rising from the depths of the lake, up through the manhole-cover-sized opening in the ice, just visible in the night dark . . .

'My God,' Dustin said, his breath hitching. 'No . . .'

It was a child.

It was *his* child.

The fishing rod fell from Dustin's numb fingers, to join the ice saw and the entire world in the inky black. All that he could see was that tow-headed child, *his* entire world, his boy, rising from the water, eyes open and bright and *alive.*

He scrambled to the edge and plunged his hands into the lake, gasping at the cold, and yes, now he could *feel* his boy. He was *real*, he was alive, and Dustin didn't care how, though a small part of him thanked his own father for hearing his prayer to help catch a fish and saying, *I can do you one better, kiddo.*

The first of his boy to break the surface was a lock of blond hair, the one that always fell in a perfect curl across his forehead when he slept. Then came the rest of his head, and a small part of Dustin realized this was his boy before the sickness—he still had the hair, still had the baby fat to hide the sharp angles of his skull. His grinning face shone in delight at the sight of his father rescuing him from death.

'Daddy!'

'Son,' Dustin said, and now he was sobbing, could barely breathe as he pulled his dead son impossibly from a lake in Maine where he'd never been in life. 'S-son, it's okay, I got you, I got you, it's okay—'

'It's so cold over there, Daddy.'

Those words . . . Dustin gasped. They were the same words—the last words—his boy had said to him in that never-ending white hospital room. The last words he'd spoken. Dustin had awoke, disoriented, in a chair beside his son's hospital bed, thinking there was a dead fish in his hand, and then—

I don't wanna go, Daddy. It's so cold over there.

Dustin had scooted closer to the bed, taking his boy's tiny hand in both of his own, and his mind had screamed, *Over there?! What does he mean? What can he mean?!* and then his son's eyes had closed forever and Dustin's world had turned cold.

And here was his son now, free from the shackles of his sickness, of his death, climbing from the depths of a lake a hundred miles from his grave, saying those same words, and it was enough to make his mind cleave in two. Like that distant horizon, riven in two perfect halves of sky and snow. Dustin didn't know on which side he now lay.

But still he lifted the boy from the ice. Surely none of that mattered—all that mattered was that he had his son back. He had his *son* back.

The pyjamas the boy wore were soaked through, and his snow-white skin seemed to shine through the thin cotton. But he wasn't shivering. It was this last fact that finally broke through Dustin's frozen mind. That lake water had to be near freezing. Hypothermia? Was that it?

No, stupid, the voice said. *Children don't just come crawling from lakes.*

But he didn't care. He held his boy, his precious child. He looked into those beautiful blue eyes and he sobbed in relief, sobbed like he never had at the funeral. He sobbed and he said, 'Son ... son, Daddy's got you. Daddy loves you.'

His heart full, he pulled his son up and out of the water.

But the boy didn't stop there, didn't stay in his arms. He kept rising, the lake water dripping from his body.

He rose ... and rose ... and rose.

And then he laughed.

Dustin fell back, distantly aware of the bucket banging away on the ice.

'Son!'

He sprawled on his back, staring up at his child.

The boy had risen impossibly high. He leered down at his father from ten feet in the air, dangled above him like a marionette.

But where are the strings, Dustin? the voice insisted.

The ice beneath him began to buckle and crack.

Tink . . . tink . . . TINK—

It heaved like tectonic plates, breaking apart, the fishing hole gaping wide for something . . . something *bigger . . .*

He looked—but oh God, he did not want to look—and what he saw drew a scream from his throat, spewing frosted breath into the night air.

His boy was glowing, a shining beacon in the winter night, bathing the ice with ethereal, alien light . . . and beneath him, pushing up out of the jagged, splintered ice and emerging from the lake, was a gigantic fish of nightmarish proportions. Big, seething cheeks of scabrous flesh scraped against the ice as it broke free, a bulbous sac of a monster. Spindly needles of teeth splayed out from its gums in dense rows, teeth as long as the ice saw, wherever it lay. The thing's mouth seemed impossibly large, splitting its entire body as it gaped open, seething hungrily, engulfing Dustin in a wash of foetid breath. It smelled of death, of a horde of bloated corpses dredged from the primordial depths. Spiny fins thwapped into the air, fanning out on either side of its grotesque, fleshy body, and barbels as thick as steel cables whipped from its every surface. Above its jack-o'-lantern mouth, a large, wide-set pair of midnight-black, sightless orbs swivelled madly in their sockets, reflecting back the glow of his son far above.

And rising from a knobby ridge between its eyes, like a horn, was a sinewy stalk of flesh that snaked up high into the frigid air and propped up his boy, like a ventriloquist's arm inside its puppet.

'It's so cold, Daddy,' the thing that looked like his son said. 'Come and help me get warm.'

Dustin's scream was strangled in his throat. This could not be. Mere seconds before, he'd held his own living, breathing son in his arms. Everything he wanted in this world, dangled before him and snatched away by some impossible monster? No. He refused.

'Son'—he stretched his arms up into the night—'son, come back. Just ... climb—climb down, and ... I'll catch you. I'll catch you and keep you safe and w-warm.'

His boy looked down at him, helpless, and whimpered. Dustin's heart broke anew.

'I'll catch you, son. I'll always catch you.'

Still he whimpered.

A hot wave of stench washed over Dustin. His eyes watered, and he looked away, blocking the monstrous fish from his vision.

Above, the whimpers rose, capering into a carnival giggle.

'Grampa told me you'd never take me here. I kept begging and begging and then I died, Daddy. So Grampa took me fishing instead.'

No.

Hot tears steamed from his cheeks. His fingers found the ice saw where it lay, and he gripped it. Its metal teeth bit into his palm, a pain that sang in concert with a sudden surge of anger. It buoyed him up. Back on his feet, he turned to the fish and hefted the saw like a javelin.

'Get your fucking hands off my boy, old man.'

He ran at the yawning maw.

The ice buckled and seesawed beneath his feet, but onward Dustin charged, jabbing the tip of the saw into the beast. It stuck in the gums. His eardrums nearly burst from the thing's answering roar. Before it could flop forward and swallow him whole, he dove to one side, yanking the saw free. Loose slabs of ice bobbed as he leapt.

He stabbed and stabbed, fuelled by righteous anger, but he found nothing resembling relief. Green, bilious fish's blood splashed and steamed. The thing came dangerously close with a hideous shriek and a sudden white-hot point of pain bloomed in Dustin's chest. His knees buckled but still he remained upright, as if suspended on the same lure as his son. The taste of copper filled his mouth. He looked down, stared incomprehensively at the yellowed quill that pierced his chest.

The fish had impaled him on one of its innumerable bottom teeth.

He coughed; black blood spooled down his front.

'Son . . . son . . .' He gulped, spat more blood.

In the near distance, his tent and the sled of gear slid

down a tottering slab of ice and disappeared into the water. Before he could let the saw follow them, he gripped its polycarbonate handle and roared. His vision blotted out. He thrashed the saw into the fish's mouth, incandescent with rage, screaming at the fish and his father and the cancer and every faceless stranger at the funeral who took his boy away from him.

A *snap!* and loosening of pressure, and suddenly he lay in a heap on the ice.

Still his son hung above, laughing.

'Do you hate me, Daddy? Was Grampa right about that, too?'

The fight left him. He lay there, boneless, on the ice, half submerged in the lake. His blood seeped red blossoms all around, finally giving colour to the never-ending white.

'Son . . . son . . .'

He still held the saw—or maybe it was the giant, spear-like fang that had impaled him. Perhaps he could cut the stalk holding his boy up, hack it down like the hero in some fairy-tale. Perhaps—

The behemoth leered down at him. It hulked above, a pot-bellied furnace of death.

'WHAT DO YOU WANT FROM ME?!'

The fish bellowed back. Thick ropes of saliva hit him, burning like acid where they lay, but he was too weak to scream.

'Take me instead.' His voice was hoarse, ragged. Dead.

'Take me in his place, just—just let my child live.'

But even as he uttered these words, his boy's voice parroted them back, mocking him.

'Son . . .'

But that thing, he knew—he'd always known—was not his son.

He slumped. The saw slid between two chunks of ice and disappeared into the lake.

What was the point?

He could no longer feel his body. He no longer cared.

He'd never hold his boy again. He'd never escape this creature and he was a fool for trying. And if he did somehow outpace some ungodly leviathan? He'd freeze to death before he made the shore.

Isn't this what you want, Dustin? the voice in his head whispered. *Isn't that why you came here?*

The fish roared. He shivered violently in the putrid heat of its breath.

This is why you came out here, the voice said. *You've caught your fish.*

Yes. Yes, Dustin knew. This was the truth of Dustin fleeing from the funeral, of coming to his dead father's cabin, of his drunken retreat to the ice.

He rose to his knees, his blood still gurgling from his body and leaving his as white as the snow, and he faced the fish head-on.

No longer did his body shake. He was calm. The kaleidoscope had stilled; the voice spoke no more. He knelt and he waited for the splintered teeth of the creature to take him, all the while craning his neck to the heavens, so that he might stare into the shining eyes of his child.

Dustin was done with the cold and the grief.

He was ready to meet the horizon.

AUTHOR'S NOTE

Stories are strange creatures—far stranger, in my eyes, than the creatures I write about. "The Cold, The Grief" began over a year ago, for a different anthology entirely. Originally Dustin's child was a victim of a drunk driving accident, but I changed this later so that I could submit it to Blood Rites Horror's charity contest to raise funds for Cancer Research UK, *Parasite Gods.* It was a happy accident—the alcoholism theme felt very one-note, while the leukaemia added much-needed emotional depth.

Fast-forward to *Bitter Chills.* I wrote an entirely different story for that anthology at first (more on that later), but after learning that the anthology would not be published until a couple months *after* Christmas, I pulled my submission and sent in "The Cold, The Grief" instead.

This story is perhaps my favourite of my writing from 2020, but when I had the chance to revise and expand it for this special edition, I knew I had to. Don't get me wrong—I love the original, shorter version (which you can listen to on the podcast Into the Gloom, as narrated by

Thomas Gloom). But some readers felt cheated by the ending. It happened in a flash, Dustin seeing the monster and accepting his fate with open arms.

At its core, Dustin's story is grief horror. So I took the opportunity (with the generous help of both Roxie Voorhees and Jay Alexander) to let Dustin finally do the work he needed to do in order to process the death of his child before he's left to his fate. He wades through all five stages of grief in that final confrontation with what I'll call his grief monster. I cannot imagine what Dustin and his family would have gone through—what any parent who loses a child to cancer goes through—so I felt it was the least I could do to help him fight for closure and, finally, peace.

Ironically, my original submission to *Bitter Chills* was not so emotional—not in the slightest. It's simple gory holiday fun. I've always wanted to give it a home, but in the writing business placing seasonal holiday stories can be tough. So I was thrilled to hear that there was a Holiday Edition of this anthology in the works, because it meant that this story, "Little Billy's Naughty Christmas", would finally get its chance on the page. It's a strange story, but I rather like it. Another thank-you is in order to Jay Alexander (or rather, Jay's former self, Nick Harper, may he never rest in peace), whose insight into writing vivid gore that (hopefully) doesn't break the reader's suspension of disbelief has been of immense help throughout my writing.

I hope you enjoy both of these strange tales—though maybe not too much. For my part, I'm happy to finally put Dustin's demons to rest. Sorry for what I put you through, Dust, but you're free to roam the greatest fishing spot in Maine astride your grief monster till the rest of us have learned to give your shores a wide berth. I like to think you eventually conquered that giant angler.

Spencer Hamilton

November 2021

MY WHITE STAR

BY CARLA ELIOT

'Well, where the hell is she? We've not seen her for days.'

I slide into my friend's car, nudging a coke can and a half-eaten sandwich to the side with my trainer.

'Not a clue,' James says, turning the key in the ignition. Scarlet—James' beloved 1974 Golf GTI—wheezes and coughs before barely coming to life. 'To be honest, I'm thinking she's probably just gone off to the Lake District earlier than she planned. You know she's been saying for weeks she couldn't wait to get away.'

Martha is the female in our trio. We've all been best friends since we were kids, when we met at the musical theatre classes we used to attend, every Saturday morning. James is right; she's probably been mentioning the Lake District trip every day now since she booked it back in October. She's been running herself into the ground recently; finishing off her assignments, working her part-time job at Tina's Cafe and fitting in band practice with us—we have a pretty shit band, if I'm honest, but Martha is good on the drums and I enjoy guitar, while James is our vocalist.

It is now January and snow has been falling sporadically since the weekend. There is a strange mist that hangs in the air like smoke - dirty and curling around the town houses. I stare out at the frosted leaves of the trees in my aunt's garden, not convinced that Martha would depart now, not with it being so cold. Plus, we have our next gig in a couple of weeks time.

I am gazing at the white, sparkling plants when a sudden flash from my bedroom window catches my eye.

I glance up and there she is.

For some reason, Martha is in my bedroom, standing by the window. She is gazing out, her face passive. I can't understand how she's managed to get into my aunt's house without me noticing. It doesn't matter, I'm relieved to see her.

'James, she's here,' I say, snapping open my seat belt and flicking the door handle. I hear James yell, 'What are you talking about? Who–' before the car door slams shut.

I glance up again and wave, but Martha doesn't seem to notice me. I recognise the green bodice of the dress she's wearing. The same dress she'd worn the night of the New Years Eve party. I wonder why she's wearing it today. The glint of her hair brooch flashes again, a temporary white star in my vision.

I step and slide down the path to the front door, the icy air seeping straight through my clothes. I don't need the house key—my aunt tends to leave the door unlocked. I think she's still stuck in a time where people could be

116

trusted. The dimly lit hallway smells of Sunday roast—it always does, even when it isn't a Sunday. I can hear my aunt moving about in the kitchen, the deep tones of Barry White on the radio. She probably hasn't even heard me come back in.

I take the stairs two at a time and the smell of homely food disappears. Instead, a cloying scent hits me as soon as I reach the top of the stairs. It's as if someone has just thrown a sickly bath bomb at me. I recognise it to be Martha's perfume. It smells a lot stronger than usual, though. There is also another smell; earthy and fresh, not unpleasant.

As I head down the windowless corridor I glimpse Martha's curvy figure, through the gap between the frame and door of my bedroom. I can see that she is definitely wearing the same green dress that she wore for New Years. I find it a bit odd, particularly on a freezing day like today.

'Martha, where have you been?'

The door moans softly as I open it further and step into my room.

'Are you okay? What are you do–' My voice sticks in my throat and I freeze in the doorway.

I have a crazy urge to laugh as I glance around the empty room. I look behind the door, lift the duvet cover to check under the bed. My mound of clothes spills out of the open wardrobe, leaving no room to hide.

Martha isn't here.

But I can still smell her perfume; it lingers like a sickly fog. I breathe it in as I stand by the window, my hands clutching the sill, wondering if I'm losing my marbles.

I stare down at Scarlet, and where James still sits, waiting for me. Snow has started to fall softly on the roof of the car. I'm lost in the hypnotic motion of the flakes for a moment, as I stand in the same spot where I saw Martha, just a couple of minutes before.

A red blur of movement, to my right, suddenly catches my attention. The tip of its bushy tail and snout is camouflaged against the snowy surroundings. The fox darts quickly across the road and vanishes into one of the gardens.

Eventually the smell fades and I go back downstairs, pulling up my hood as I step outside.

I slam the car door shut, wondering what to say to James.

'What was that about?' he asks as I buckle up.

'It's really weird. I could have sworn that I saw Martha.'

'What do you mean? Saw her where?'

'In my room. Up there. In the window.' I peer up towards my bedroom window, but all I see now is the reflection of the falling snow. There is silence next to me, and I turn to James to see him staring at me, confused lines etching his pale forehead.

'And what?' he eventually says, shrugging, his hands

on the steering wheel.

'She wasn't there. God, I don't know if I'm losing my mind, but I could smell her perfume too. You know that stuff she always wears.'

'Oh yeah, that shit that smells like lilies, always hated that stuff.' He turns the key and checks his blind spot before looking back at me. 'And I don't think you're losing your marbles. I think Saturday night is catching up with you. You were wasted.'

I don't really want to talk about it anymore and I can tell James is itching to get going, so I just say, 'Yeah, you're probably right.'

He pulls out onto the narrow road and we head to his house for band practice, just the two of us.

I can't get into it that evening. It just isn't the same without Martha, and the scent of her keeps whispering around me every now and then, making it difficult to concentrate. My fingers are thick and clumsy on the chords.

I try phoning Martha a few times but it just goes through to voicemail.

James drops me back off a few hours later, telling me to get an early night. I climb the stairs, my head woozy from the couple of beers that we'd had during practice. I've not eaten anything this evening; I haven't the stomach for it.

The sound of the TV echoes out from the living room, where my aunt will spend most of the evening. I've gotten used to living here. It is different from my parents' house. Not worse, just different. I guess I don't have much choice really. They aren't coming back.

I close the door on the rest of my thoughts, knowing where they will lead, and instead, focus on the door at the end of the corridor: my bedroom.

It is slightly ajar, the darkness within spilling out, shifting with the shadows in the corridor. I flick the light switch and pause, straining my eyes to peer through the gap between the frame and the door.

I can see the outline of my bed, the hulking shape of the chest of drawers, and the window which frames the star-studded sky. But no Martha.

Once in bed, I check my phone every thirty seconds, hoping to see a text from her.

It's been three days since we last saw her. James doesn't seem concerned, and usually maybe I wouldn't be either. As I stare at the dark ceiling, the sounds of the TV floating up from below, I have to admit to myself that maybe my feelings go beyond merely being concerned about a friend. Since Saturday and the party, my thoughts have definitely gone beyond thinking about Martha as just a friend.

I have feelings for her, and maybe I'd expressed that

too openly. I am worried that I've scared her off. That I am the reason for her sudden silence.

When I'd thought that I'd seen her up in my bedroom, gazing out of the window, my heart had thudded, excitedly. I look over at the empty space now, and consider what it must have been. *A hallucination? My anxious brain just showing me what it thought I wanted to see?* God knows; that had happened plenty of times before, with my parents.

I think of them now, cold and still in the ground. Insects crawling over their rotting bodies, nibbling at their papery white skin. I squeeze my eyes shut, trying to stop the torrent of unwanted images, and eventually I fall asleep.

A harsh light filters through my eyelids, pulling me from the blackness of sleep. My eyes flicker and I struggle to fully open them for a moment, temporarily blinded by the slice of white light. I feel as if I've hardly slept and my foggy brain is trying to remember if I'd closed the curtains. I finally manage to open my eyes, mumbling and pulling the duvet up to my shoulders. I then notice that the room is dark, that it's the middle of the night.

And there's a figure by the window.

I can see that I did leave the curtains open, so the moon's milky light is pouring into the room and shimmers off of Martha's dark auburn hair. Her dress shines like a pool of green silk. I can make out the shape of her pale calves, so white against her black stiletto shoes.

'Martha?' I mumble.

The slice of light cuts through my vision, again, and I hold up my arm to protect my eyes.

As I squint and stare at the back of her head, I distinguish the source of the light.

Her hair brooch glitters and glimmers, the moon's light bouncing off of it and splitting the darkness. I remember seeing the trembling glow of it in the window today. It was what had caught my attention in the first place.

'Martha, what are you doing here? Are you okay?' I wonder if I'm dreaming or maybe hallucinating, again.

The hair brooch flashes, blinding me. A bright, twinkling star, encompassing everything.

I shut my eyes and when I open them again, she's gone.

I am woken, again, by the flashing light.

I sit up immediately, wanting to clarify—for my own sanity, if nothing else—that what I am seeing must be real. I also don't want to lose a moment of time with Martha, even if she is an illusion.

But I'm surprised to see that she isn't standing by the window. After glancing around and scanning the shadows, I can see that my room is empty.

The flashing, however, continues, a wedge of crisp light signalling for me to notice it; Martha's hair brooch.

I push the duvet to the side and swing my legs out of bed. I edge slowly towards the window, carefully, afraid that if I move too fast or blink for too long, the light will vanish. The flicker changes as I move closer. Grows faint and shifts position. When I'm by the window, I grip the sill, fearful that the illusive light has gone. But then, leaning forward, head lowered in disappointment, I see it.

Martha's hair brooch winks up at me, reflecting the moon's beam, from behind the radiator. My heart stops, at the same time as my brain runs frantically.

How has Martha's hair brooch ended up behind the radiator, in my bedroom? The last time I saw Martha wearing it was the night of the party. I've not seen her since Saturday, yet here is her brooch. So where is Martha? Why was she in my bedroom?

I slip my hand between the wall and the radiator. I notice the tremble of my fingers and hope that I won't cause the brooch to get lodged, or worse, that it doesn't disappear before I am able to retrieve it.

But my fingers touch the cold sharp stones of the brooch, and it doesn't disintegrate and disappear; it is very real. I carefully pull it out, and once it is free I hold it in the palms of my hands, like I'm holding a very precious and rare bird.

It is exquisite. Just looking at it brings back the memory of Saturday night. Staring down at Martha as she laughed at something that I said, the brooch catching the light and twinkling like a star in her hair. But it wasn't as beautiful as the stars in Martha's eyes. As she'd stared up at me, with her open smile.

I had fallen in love with her that night. And at the time I had thought that she felt the same. I was certain of it. Now, I don't know . . .

The memory continues, snippets of moments, although I don't recall experiencing them. An avalanche of emotions and thoughts suddenly engulf me.

It's the night of the party.

But not how I remember it.

I can see myself, passed out on James' sofa at his parents' house. There are empty bottles and cans littering practically every surface of the living room. Greasy pizza boxes are piled up on the coffee table. Almost everyone has gone home. Just a couple of people still loiter in the white garden, smoking.

Something is digging into the upper flesh of my arm. But it's not my arm, because I am looking at my sleeping form on the sofa. I glance down and see a pale, slender arm. Painted black nails at the end of an elegant hand.

I realise that I'm Martha.

Somebody is gripping Martha's arm. I can see the nails biting into the soft flesh.

I yank myself free of the vicious grasp and look up.

My blood turns cold.

The look in James' eyes is frightening. I've never seen him like this.

I step back, widening the gap between us, trying to distance myself from the rage that is emanating from him.

'What do you mean, 'what am I doing?'' My voice is brittle; anger barely masking my fear.

'You've been grazing yourself up against Kyle all night, you're acting like a cheap slut.' James' words are full of so much venom that saliva shoots out from his mouth and I feel drops of it hit my face.

'How dare you speak to me like that? I like Kyle. What's that got to do with you? I think you need to get it out of your head that something is going to happen between you and me, because it isn't.'

I turn away, but James grabs my arm, again. He pulls it so hard that it feels as though he almost yanks it out of its socket.

'I've been telling you how I feel about you. That I want us to be together.' James' face is too close to mine, his eyes searing into me. I force myself to keep eye contact, hoping that my next words will hit home.

'Just because you feel that way and want those things, James, it doesn't mean I do. And I'm telling you now: I. Don't.'

Out of nowhere he grabs my chin, snapping my head upwards. He's gone too far. I swing my arm and it strikes the side of his face. It's a clumsy blow, but it does the trick and he lets me go, stumbling back.

I run past Kyle who is still sound asleep, stepping over the empty party poppers, their colourful guts spilled across the carpet. I rush through to the kitchen, and spotting the last few stragglers in the garden, I stop, take a deep breath, before going out to join them.

I don't usually smoke, but I accept when somebody offers me one. I need to calm down and I hope the cigarette will help me do that. I gaze up at the sky, trying to focus on the stars, but all the time listening out for James, hoping that he doesn't follow me outside.

My breath clouds, and I watch it as it mingles with the cold air before vanishing into the night. One person leaves, and then another. Midnight seems so long ago, now. I can still taste Kyle's lips on mine. I hug my arms, my flesh as pale as the snow. I've left my coat inside, but I daren't go back in to retrieve it.

I don't want to go home. I'm too strung up. The person I want to talk to is Kyle, but he is currently dead to the world. I need to tell him about James. About all the messages he's been sending me. The phone calls. His never-ending insisting that we are meant to be together. It is becoming frightening. James has been my best friend for so long, but now, it is like I don't even know him. He's become obsessed.

I hope that Kyle will believe me, when I tell him. I think he will. Tonight I felt something with him. A connection. I am apprehensive about taking things further with him, because I don't want to lose another friend. But I need to confide in him.

I suddenly have an idea. I'll walk to Kyle's house. It's not far. His aunt won't mind me waiting there until Kyle recovers and returns home. Besides, if his aunt is asleep I can always just slip quietly into the house; the front door is generally always kept unlocked.

A couple of minutes later I grind out the cigarette, say my goodbyes to the couple of people that are left, and take the path *around the side of the house, leaving my coat.*

The roads are quiet. Parked cars are coated in snow. The frosty tarmac sparkles in the moonlight, breathtakingly beautiful. I'm careful as I walk, trying not to slip on patches of ice. The houses stand silently watching me as I pass by, their strings of twinkling Christmas lights offering little comfort. The sound of my stiletto heels clipping along the pavement is unnerving. I'm relieved when I finally reach Kyle's house.

At the door, I pull out from my bag my favourite bottle of perfume. I stink of cigarette smoke and I don't want Kyle's aunt to smell it, although I doubt she will still be awake. I spray a cloud of perfume and let it settle on me, before slipping the bottle back in my bag and stepping inside the house. The sound of the TV is spilling out from the living room. I pop my head round the door, intending to let Kyle's aunt know that I'm here, but she is just a shadowy, curled up form on the sofa. Her tiny snores confirm to me that she is fast asleep.

I tiptoe up the stairs and tread quietly along the dark corridor. The door moans when I push it open. I quickly stop it opening further—not wanting to wake Kyle's aunt—and slip into the room.

I don't turn on a light, feeling safer in the dark: my black cave, protecting me from the wilderness. I sit on the edge of Kyle's bed for a while. I'm exhausted, but I'd feel uncomfortable just sprawling out on his duvet. Besides, I'm too anxious to sleep. There's the sound of a car, driving slowly by, but then silence resumes outside.

The moon is pouring milky light into the room, and then I

notice that it's snowing, again, tiny flakes floating softly down. I get to my feet, and go to stand by the window to watch as the world transforms. I admire the glistening gardens and watch the piles of snow rise on window sills and chimneys. Out of nowhere a fleeting streak of red catches my eye. I admire the fox as she slinks across the road and disappears into a neighbour's garden, leaving little footprints behind; tiny hearts in the snow.

I notice then the fresh footprints along the path, just below the window and disappearing by the front door.

Something disturbs the silence; a footfall on the stairs.

Kyle?

I instantly feel my shoulders relax as I listen to him carefully making his way along the corridor, towards the bedroom.

I don't turn as I hear him enter the room, the small sigh of the door hinges giving him away. I'm thinking about what to say to him. How I can tell him. I know that once the words are out there will be no going back. I will be crossing a line and potentially breaking the friendship between the three of us, forever. But maybe it had already been wrecked anyway, by James.

I realise I must look like a ghostly figure, just standing silently by the window, so I decide to say, 'I'm sorry that I came here, without asking. I just really needed to talk to you about James.'

'What do you have to say about James?'

I whirl around to face James, my heart in my throat.

I know right then that things aren't going to end well. The look in James' hard eyes is terrifying. They seem to glow in the shadowy room. I have a gut feeling that I'm not going to leave this bedroom. That I'm never going to breathe in the night air, again.

I open my mouth to scream, hoping that Kyle's aunt will hear me, but James is too quick. His fist strikes the side of my temple. The blow sends me toppling sideways. My head feels like it has been snapped from my neck and a blaze of stars fill my vision. I am vaguely aware of my hair coming loose. I hear the clatter of my hair brooch as it hits the radiator, before I sink to the floor and into oblivion.

I was wrong. I thought that I'd never breathe in the night air again, but the earthy, fresh scent of it tickles my nostrils, gently nudging me awake.

I've always loved the smell of the night. Now though, my senses are dulled by the coldness seeping through my dress. I open my eyes and I'm stunned to see the canopy of skeletal branches above me, dusted in snow.

I realise then, why I'm so cold. I'm lying on a blanket of snow. My brain is fuzzy, so I can't work out how I've ended up here.

Then a figure slides above me, blocking out the trees.

James.

I instantly remember what he did in the bedroom and I begin to scream.

His fingers wrap around my neck, until it sounds like the scream is being squeezed from a bottle that is nearly empty.

I claw at his arms. Kick out with my legs. Wriggle and fling myself upwards, flopping back onto the ground, like a struggling, desperate fish out of water. Eventually, the fight in me dissipates, and I allow myself to sink into the snow. Allow the coldness to absorb me completely.

I think that a never-ending nothingness will override everything else, and I'm grateful for it.

Except, it doesn't come.

Instead, I'm suspended in the air, staring down at my frozen, lifeless body. My face is pale, as white as the snow, my hair a burning halo, spread out like fiery tendrils.

Everything is still.

The stillness extends, silence with it, as if I am peering down at a photograph.

Then suddenly, James rises. I watch as he grabs my ankles and begins to drag me across the white earth.

He disappears from the scene, along with my dead body, and all that remains are the swirling patterns in the snow that I'd created with my thrashing legs when I'd tried to save myself, and the imprint of my body; the shape of a snow angel.

My tears fall on the brooch in my hands.

I'm on the floor in my bedroom, back against the radiator, and I stay in that position for a long time. I hug my knees, head bowed, and weep into my arms. I don't drop the brooch; I cling onto it, wrapping my hand around it—ignoring the bite of the sharp stones against the palm of my hand—hoping to catch another glimpse of Martha.

When there is nothing, the anger begins to bubble inside of me. My ears roar and my whole body shakes with a frightening energy. I slowly get to my feet, legs wobbly, and trudge to the bedside drawers, eyes on my mobile phone.

A few seconds later, the text is sent. I hadn't typed a message; the photo of the brooch would be enough. I knew that he would come.

A couple of hours later, I finally see a hunched figure, making his way carefully along the icy pavement, on the opposite side of the road. It doesn't surprise me that he hasn't come in his car. Walking is more discreet.

The morning is dark, just a thin, watery streak of light is beginning to appear gradually across the sooty sky, as the rising sun fights to be seen.

I'm still holding the brooch, carefully now, like it's a snowflake in my hand, standing by the window. As if sensing my presence, James looks up. He doesn't wave, and although his features are dark, I can tell he isn't smiling. He pauses briefly, at the edge of the pavement, and I wonder if he is thinking of turning back around, not ready to face me. But, keeping his eyes fixed on me, he steps forward, onto the road and begins to cross.

A cloud shifts—its shadow a passing ghost on the road—and the sun is briefly able to expel some warmth. The yellow light beams down, catching the stones of the brooch. It flashes in my hands; a pulsing, shimmering star.

An awful screeching sound causes me to look up from

the brooch, and the first thing I notice is that James has stopped moving. His arm is up, as if shielding his eyes from a harsh light. The next thing I am aware of is the fast blur of movement to my right - as the car tries to slow down, tyres spinning, struggling to find purchase on the slippery road.

Then the rest happens heart-wrenchingly fast, and even after what James did, I wish that I could turn back time, just thirty seconds before he took that fatal step in front of the car. It was a devastating scene that succinctly demonstrated how life can be snatched away from us in just a blink of an eye. It was also a beautiful and ironic example of the butterfly effect, holding Martha's brooch in my hand, like it, itself, was a precious butterfly, as it reflected the sun and flashed brightly, a wedge of light, temporarily blinding James.

It happens fast, but I read every slow, horrified expression that crosses James' face as he registers the car, too late. His eyes widen, mouth contorting in pain, as metal hits flesh.

I am certain his eyes meet mine, briefly, as the impact flings him into the frigid air.

I imagine that I hear the crunch of his bones as he lands on the bonnet of the car, before rolling off onto the icy tarmac, a crumpled, lifeless form.

Only when it is done, does the brooch in my hand stop twinkling, and the sun disappears behind the dark clouds once more. Justice has been done.

Nearly a year later . . .

The snow is falling, again, silent, gentle and commemorative; almost symbolic as I kneel by the gravestone.

I try not to think of Martha, below the earth, where she'd already spent so long after James had murdered her. I try to think of the way she was the last time I saw her alive - eyes shining as she smiled up at me.

I no longer have her brooch, it's either with the police, or otherwise, has been returned to Martha's parents after the investigation came to a close.

After James' sudden death, his parents found strands of red hair in the boot of his car, along with a shovel. As Martha had been reported missing by that point, this raised suspicions. When I handed the brooch into the police and told them what I knew - omitting the bit out about seeing Martha's ghost - it didn't take them long to find James' distinctive red Golf GTI on the traffic cameras. The last camera that picked up Scarlet was on the road that led to the nature reserve, just ten minutes from my aunt's house. A day later, the sniffer dogs found Martha's body.

I wish I still had her hair brooch, some part of her that I could hold in my hands and keep forever. But as I study Martha's name on the headstone in front of me, I know that she's already given me a gift.

I can still remember how soft and warm her lips had been on mine. Right now, I am breathing in the icy air, thankful to be alive. Who knew what James would have done if he'd managed to cross the road.

Some time later, I rise from my knees, the snow already settled on my clothes so that I blend into the winter white world. On my way to the gate of the cemetery, I make another stop. I place a bunch of red roses in between my parents' headstones; a smudge of blood on the glistening, white snow. I say a silent prayer - the first I've ever made - and briefly glance up, towards the pearly white sky.

As I do, I'm sure that I see something flash, immediately reminding me of Martha and her hair brooch.

A twinkling star; a sign, or maybe a farewell, from Martha, or my parents, I don't know - perhaps it's from all three.

It is gone in an instant, but I know it was there, just for me.

My white star.

AUTHOR'S NOTE

One evening, I had a lucid dream in which I was walking down a gloomy corridor towards a door that was slightly ajar. Peering through the gap, I saw the outline of a woman, standing by a window with her back to me. I opened the door wider, ready to speak to her, but there was no one there, and my dream abruptly changed to a different scene. I was blinded by a bright, white light, and behind the light, there was the same woman I'd seen before; I couldn't decipher much about her; all I knew was that she was wearing a green dress and black stilettos. From these two fragments of my dream, I was inspired to write My White Star.

As soon as I woke up, I wrote down notes on these two scenes, and then I began to think about how I could link them together and turn them into a story. Where was the bright light emanating from? Who was the woman? What had happened to her? And what was she trying to tell me? I was so inspired and excited about where these ideas could go, I got to working on the story straight away. I wrote the first draft of My White Star over two evenings.

Since the birth of this story, I think that my writing has

evolved somewhat, but this one will always hold a special place in my heart. I really hope that you, the reader, like it as much as I do. Many thanks to the editor, Jay, for accepting "My White Star", which was my first story to be published.

Carla Eliot

THE KILLER SNOWMAN

CASS OAKLEY

THE KILLER SNOWMAN
BY CASS OAKLEY

Marie dug a carrot out the fridge and took it outside to where her family were constructing a snowman next to the slide the children were too old to play on now. The dog bounded alongside her, throwing snow into the air. Marie whistled him back over as he tried to cock his leg on the swings on the other side of the garden.

'Mom! Mom! Mom!' shouted Ted. 'Quick, I'm gonna drop his head!'

'Oh what makes you think this snowman is a boy?' Marie ruffled his hair and helped heave the snow head on top of the body whilst Ted rolled his eyes.

'My friend at school, mom, my friend says that when it gets dark snowmen come to life,' said Jimmy.

'They're not alive, idiot,' scowled Ted.

'Hey, be nice to your brother. Who said that, Jim?'

'One of my friends said their gran said it. You have to walk three times around the snowman and chant I believe. And then, right mom, and then you get to go on adventures with them.'

Marie glanced at her wife, smiling. 'Shall we try it?'

The three of them began to walk around the freshly built snowman, whilst Ted scoffed and pressed coal into the snowman's face.

'Do you not wanna go on adventures, Ted? Are you too old for that, my little cherub?' cooed Lindsay after they stopped chanting. She pinched his cheek and laughed. 'Come on, let's go inside and warm up ready for a magical adventure.'

Marie pulled her pyjamas on as Lindsay got into bed. She leant over and gave her a prod. 'I guess I'll close the curtains then!'

'Oh go on, be a darling,' said Lindsay, burrowing into the thick duvet.

Marie scoffed but went over to the window to shut the curtains. There was a flurry of snow falling again and she watched it fall by the street lamppost for a while. She gave a start when she realised the snowman they'd built early was staring up at her. She chuckled, noticing it was just the light off the lamp creating odd shadows as it reflected off the snow. The snowman had slouched somewhat and appeared to be leaning casually against the swings. She pulled the curtains closed and snuggled into bed.

Marie slouched down to the kitchen the next morning to let the dog outside. 'Eurgh!' she exclaimed as her socked foot slid in a puddle of water. 'Remember to wipe your feet, guys!' she yelled back up the stairs, opening the back door. There was a trail of water in the kitchen and she popped the kettle on whilst she mopped it up with a tea towel. She stood at the window watching the dog sniff around the garden. He'd already made a large trail in the snow leading up the patio steps. He barked at the snowman at the top of the steps and Marie knocked the window to make him stop. She squeezed at the tea bag and moved to put it in the bin. There was a rap at the window. She turned sharply but no one was there. The dog was stood with his hackles raised, a low growl forming in his throat. Marie went to the back door as there was a yelp and called him in, presuming there was some early morning joggers in the gully behind the garden. She glanced at the snowman, one of the kids must have moved his coal-made mouth into a frown and she rolled her eyes. The dog darted into the kitchen soaking wet and she groaned.

'Silly dog!' Marie reached for another towel to dry the dog off. There was a rap at the window again. 'Damn kids!' The dog began barking and Marie tried to hush him. She opened the back door again and the dog cowered in the corner of the kitchen whining. 'Some help you are, boy!' She scanned the ground by the window and saw little bits of coal. She looked back at the snowman who was missing a few bits of his mouth; it made him look very angry. 'Really funny, you little shits, go do something productive with your time!' She tried to make her voice stern enough to carry it over the fence. She went back inside and called family down to eat breakfast, going back to drying off the dog.

Ted came skidding into the kitchen, his hair sticking up at odd angles. 'Whoa, the snowman is gone!' He pointed out the window, his mouth agape.

'Don't mess about this morning, I'm not in the mood!' said Marie, plonking the box of cereal on the breakfast bar.

'No, but mom, it's really gone . . . '

'What did I just say?' Marie's voice began to rise just as there was a knock at the back door. She exchanged a glance with her son, who shrugged. Marie walked towards the door with apprehension. It creaked as she opened it to find the snowman there, piercing coal eyes boring down at her, its arms made of sticks reached out for her. Marie slammed the door as a scream pushed its way up her throat. Ted dropped the box of cereal as the door began to rattle on its hinges. The dog was going wild as Marie yelled at Ted to get back upstairs. The door burst open as the rest of the family thundered down the stairs to see what was happening.

'Back! Back!' gasped Marie, as they all huddled at the bottom of the stairs. The wooden arms grabbed the dog as he tried to dart past. Marie screamed again but reached out for her contorting dog. The snowman leant with its icy, gaping mouth and took a chunk out of the wriggling animal. It dropped the limp corpse and turned its attention to Marie, who could only stand and stare as the red and white coldness embraced her.

AUTHOR'S NOTE

'Short, sweet, and full of potential'—a summary of reviews for 'The Killer Snowman'.

When I was first approached about this special Holiday Edition of *Bitter Chills*, I was ecstatic—I could finally expand on my very short story and have it fulfil that potential everyone kept talking about.

However, on reflection, I realised my little snowman tale was perfect with all its imperfections. I can always look back fondly on this short story as my first published work, and I hope you enjoy it all the same.

Cass Oakley

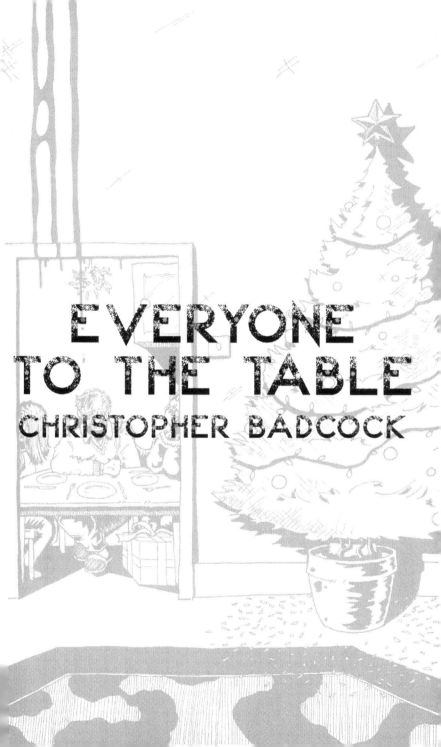

EVERYONE
TO THE TABLE
CHRISTOPHER BADCOCK

EVERYONE TO THE TABLE

BY CHRISTOPHER BADCOCK

I decided Christmas dinner would be the best time to do it.

Everyone to the table.

That's what mum always shouted from the kitchen whenever she started plating up. She said the same thing every day at around 5.15pm, but it was only ever the youngest twins who took their seats at the table, and me, of course. Dad, Jack and Byron would fetch their plates and sit in the lounge; that's where the TV was.

Christmas dinner was the only meal we all shared together at the table. That's why I chose to do it on that day. To kill them all.

I wouldn't have been able to drag my brothers in from the lounge, let alone my dad. And I'm not sure why, but I just felt like we all needed to be together when it happened. To be close to each other, having a good time, before they all died. That's what Christmas is all about, right? Not dying—I guess people do die at Christmas, though—but being together, being happy and all that sort of thing. I don't know—I mean, I'm just a kid. But it also meant they'd be together afterwards too, like when families have a big crypt, or a mum and dad love each other very much and get buried next to each other in the graveyard. They'd all be together. The house would be the crypt.

After it was all done—I put the poison in mum's fruit cake so they could enjoy all three courses first—I played with my new Commando Joe and watched the snow piling up in the garden. After a while, I got bored watching the Mackie kids and their mum making a snowman, so I sat in dad's spot on the sofa and watched Kevin set traps for the Wet Bandits on the TV.

It was good because I was like him now, I was *Home Alone*, sort of. I wasn't completely alone, but if a couple of burglars showed up like they did in the movie, my family wouldn't be able to help me, so I was pretty much on my own.

I got up and picked a candy cane from the tree when the ad breaks started—one of the green and white ones because I hate the red and white ones—then I went into the kitchen to fetch some popcorn. As I walked through the dining room though, I noticed their faces had started to sag. Their jaws all looked baggy, and their chins were nearly touching their chests. It reminded me a little of when dad would fall asleep watching the TV, but their mouths were so wide, it was like they were screaming.

That bothered me. It got worse over the next few days, to the point where I was sure I could hear their screams, because that's what it looked like. It looked like they were screaming, even though they were all dead.

And I didn't know what to do.

So, I sewed their mouths shut. I couldn't take it anymore, the constant yelling in my head. It sounded like they were scared, scared worse than Elma had been that time we all rode the Terror Train at Cratchford Fair and the green zombie jumped out of the coffin at the final corner. It sounded like they were in pain too, like when you have to visit the dentist and have a tooth out. Or even both, like a scared-pain, like if someone with a scary face jumped out of a bush and started stabbing you with a big knife in your chest.

I didn't like it.

And I didn't know what to do.

I hadn't scared them; I hadn't caused them any pain either, I'd made sure of that. They didn't have any right to make me feel guilty, to look like they'd been the victims of a bad person, a scary-faced person with a knife in a dark park. That wasn't me, I'm not a monster, and it wasn't fair that they were making me feel that way. Their deaths were supposed to change that. Killing them was supposed to make me feel better, but it was making me feel worse.

The younger twins got all of the attention because they could still do the puppy-dog face and said cute things all the time that made mum and dad laugh. The older twins got all of the glory because they were the best at sports and were doing good in their exams at school. But me, the middle kid who killed his twin in the womb, I got nothing. Just guilt, guilt that mum and dad forced on me, and my brothers did too—Jack and Byron were old enough to understand what had happened, but Elma and Corinne weren't—and it just wasn't fair, it hadn't been fair . . . but now it was. Now I didn't have to feel guilty about what happened to Millie—that was her name, my twin, the one I ate when we were both in mum's womb. I don't even know how I could've done that anyway, I didn't have any teeth until after I was born, but I heard my parents use a word, it was *consume*, and when I looked it up I found out it's the word you use when you eat something.

And I didn't know what to do.

Until I decided to kill them all.

It took months of planning, but I guess the thought had maybe been there for longer than that, I'm not one of those psycho-analysers, so I don't know, but it was probably there from the very beginning; for all I know it really was my fault that Millie died in the womb, I don't know, I'm just a kid, I don't remember feeling hungry when I was in there, I don't remember any of it.

What happened then, and what happened this Christmas, none of it's my fault. My parents were adults, they were supposed to protect me, they were supposed to love me no matter what, that's how it is in the movies. They never loved me though, they just pretended like the girls do with their dolls, but I could tell. I'm a kid, but I'm not stupid. I knew it by the way they treated me so differently compared to my brothers and sisters, I knew it by the way they always bought a gift for Millie on our birthday and at Christmas, even though she was never here to open them. They always said she was here with us. The presents were never opened though, they just put them away in the closet in their room. I know that because I found them one year when I was searching for my own presents, I wanted to know if they'd bought me the Captain Pike that all of my friends were getting. They had, but they'd also bought Millie a Windy Cindy, this stupid baby doll that farted and giggled and cost loads more than my Captain Pike did. I got in trouble when they found out, they knew it was me who'd opened it, and I got grounded for a whole week, it wasn't fair!

This year they got her a *Molly & Me* house and stables. I know because I opened it up after dinner, and those things cost a fortune. They spent more on her than they did on me, again.

It wasn't just the presents though, I knew by their eyes. I know I'm just a dumb kid, but I know eyes, I've heard grown-ups say you can read eyes and I think they're right. I think that's one of the first things you learn when you're just a baby. Someone can be smiling, but their eyes aren't smiling, their eyes can be really unhappy.

Their eyes don't show me anything now, though. After I sewed their mouths shut to stop the screaming, it wasn't long before I had to do the same to their eyes. When the screaming stopped, the staring started. Whenever I walked through the dining room they'd watch me. Last Monday, I was sure that dad's eyes followed me from the lounge to the kitchen. I didn't see them move, but he was looking right at me when I came into the room, and when I got to the other side of the room, he was still looking at me.

I thought things would get better once I did what I did, but I'm only a kid, I live pretty much day to day, I don't really plan for the future. Only for the summer holidays, and what I want for my birthday and Christmas, I don't think about how every day is going to be.

And I don't know what to do.

Aunt Sally keeps calling and leaving messages about the party we were supposed to be going to at Aunt Cara's in the new year. I spoke to her once, told her mum and dad were out and they'd left their phones at home, but it's been two weeks now and the party's next weekend. She'll want to speak with mum soon, from the sound of her messages I know she's already worrying. She never lets things go either—stupid Sally—she'll catch a train if she has to, I know she will, and if I don't answer the door she'll call the police.

And I don't know what to do.

A few days ago, I had a bowl of Sweetie Wheaties for breakfast, and I sat at the table with the rest of them, like I've been doing every morning. But Dad had moved. He and Elma had switched places, I was sure of it, I remembered where all of them were sat because my seat was always empty, and I knew who was next to me and who I was looking at. But they were in different chairs, like they got up while I was sleeping, like they were trying to play a trick on me. I thought they might still be alive, maybe I hadn't given them enough and they were all pretending to be dead, but then I remembered about the eyes and the mouths. There was no way they could've stayed quiet while I sewed them up, especially the girls, they screamed the house down if you just pulled their hair. They were definitely in different chairs though, and I don't know how. I don't know why.

And I don't know what to do.

Not last night, but the night before, I was lying in bed reading my *Fallout Phil* comic—it's a few weeks old now, I haven't left the house since before Christmas day so I don't even know if Phil saved Sharlene Shakes from the evil monster, Gargantua—and I heard noises coming from downstairs; they were coming from the dining room. It sounded like knives and forks on plates, like they were all eating. When I came downstairs the next morning, there was a stain on Jack's shirt that hadn't been there before. I knew it hadn't been there, because he was sat opposite me at the table, and I'd been flicking Wheaties at him each morning, trying to get them to land in the pocket on the front of his shirt. It was some kind of sauce, I think, but it was red, so it could've been blood, or cranberry or ketchup, maybe.

And I don't know what to do.

Last night was the worst. Last night I didn't hear any of them downstairs.

I heard something else.

It was a baby crying in the hallway. I could hear it moaning like the girls used to moan when they were just babies and they wanted their dummies. It was moving too, not walking or anything, babies can't walk, but I think it was shuffling along the floor, like a soldier behind enemy lines. I could hear it on the carpet. It started at the top of the stairs and was getting closer and closer to my room, but then I fell asleep.

And I don't know what to do.

I think the baby might come again tonight. But this time I think the baby might reach my door and get into my bedroom, even though I've jammed one of the dining room chairs under the handle. I don't think it'll make any difference.

And I don't know what to do.

I think the baby is my twin. I think the baby is Millie. And I think mum and dad were right all along. She's always been here with us.

AUTHOR'S NOTE

There isn't always a clear route to an idea, or at least one you can accurately recall, but I can share with you exactly how the idea came about for this story.

It was Christmas 2019, and I was enjoying my annual viewing of *Home Alone*, a movie that I refuse to watch in any month other than December. It's those people, the ones who watch Christmas movies in May, or sing George Michael in August: they're the ones to watch out for; they're the real evil in this world.

Anyway, the film reminded me of a silly prank my auntie Wendy would play on her husband David many years ago; she'd hide in the house somewhere, with a knife (yes, that's right) and wait for him to get home from work. On one occasion she patiently waited for a fair while, refusing to move from her hiding spot, to the point where David actually believed he was alone in the house. After making himself something to eat, having a drink, and sitting down to read and watch TV for a while, David went upstairs and a knife-wielding Wendy jumped out at him, scaring him half to death.

My younger brother and I loved hearing David tell us

this story when we were younger.

I thought it would be good if *Home Alone* was flipped on its head in a similar way and the family were actually there, just hiding, waiting in a wardrobe somewhere with knives and other lethal utensils, ready to jump out and scare an unsuspecting Macauley Culkin.

I thought that might be funny. But I don't write comedy.

So, I followed the thread a little more, and I decided it would be pretty good if the family were there, but just . . . dead.

I began drafting this idea, thinking the kid would get home from school and the family would have been murdered and buried in the back garden, or stowed away in the attic perhaps. The kid would live like a king for a while, disobeying all the rules until the murderer showed up again.

But as with all ideas, it's always good to interrogate them, to turn them around, twist them up, and ask questions of them to see if there are any interesting answers.

So, I asked myself the question, what if the kid was the murderer?

"Everyone to the Table" was the answer.

Christopher Badcock

THE CHRISTMAS EVE

CARMILLA YUGOV

THE CHRISTMAS EVE

BY CARMILLA YUGOV

I

I took a quick look outside my window. This didn't seem good at all.

The snow didn't show any signs of stopping. Three days! I was becoming a little nervous. Earlier, when I was a kid, this didn't seem so bad. In fact, there was something strangely calming about these storms. Just sitting inside, in front of a huge fireplace in the living room, listening to the music from the radio, while unwrapping the presents . . . Once, this house was full of life.

But not anymore. Today, it was just me. And, the snowstorm made me feel worried. What would I do if I got stuck here for a long time, without anyone around to help me? I felt sick. *I don't want to die here, not like this. Get stuck in my own house and starve to death, I don't want to.*

Shut up! I told myself. I took a deep breath.

The wind outside was *howling*. The light bulb in my study was flickering from time to time. *I swear to God, if the electricity goes out, I'll go crazy in here.*

The telephone was still working, but who could I call?

It had been ten years since Mom and Dad died in a skiing accident.

It had been two years since Peter Watts, the only person I had ever gotten close to since the loss of my parents, left me for someone else.

It's funny how life can be so cruel sometimes. No one knew how lonely I really was. Me, the great Miss Dolores 'Dee' Bates: a movie star, beautiful, young, well-respected and loved by everyone...

But that was just on the surface. No one actually *cared* about the 'great' Miss Bates. *Nobody.*

Just as I was thinking this, something unimaginable happened.

The phone rang.

II

'Umm . . . Hello?' a voice said. A *familiar* voice. My legs turned into liquid all of sudden; I had to sit down.

'Is anyone there? I'm looking for Miss Dolores.'

'Yes, it's me—' I was out of breath, but somehow I cleared my throat, and continued. 'Pete . . . ? Is that . . . ?'

A smile on the other side of the telephone line. 'Yes, it's me! God, it's been so long.'

My face immediately turned into a rather angry expression. *Sure, it's been a long time since you ruined my life, mister.*

'What do you want?' I didn't bother to be nice. Even now, I was still upset about everything.

'Yeah, listen, I . . . ' He breathed, as if he was about to bring me some bad news. 'I need your help, Dolores. Actually, *we* need your help.'

Well, the assumption about the bad news wasn't wrong, all right. Funny how the people who hurt and abandoned you have the guts to come back and ask for *help*!

I swallowed hard.

'Who are *we*, Peter?' I could already assume who he

160

was talking about, but I still hoped it wasn't who I thought it was.

'Me and Tamara. Yes, I know how this sounds, but we really need your help. We were on our way to Cot Castle for the Christmas holidays, but this weather slowed us down. The blizzard is going to get worse during the night, and we won't be able to make it to the hills with the car. And, because I know you lived nearby, I thought maybe. . . Look, I'll pay you, that really isn't a problem. All we need is a room, just for one night. Then we'll be back on the road in the morning. Okay? We'll stay out of your way, I promise you that. Please, Dolores. Just one night, that's all.'

Oh, well, well. Sniff, sniff, how sad I am to hear that. So sad that you and your little missus aren't able to make it to your dream vacation place, you have no idea. It breaks my heart so much, almost as much as you broke mine when you left me for that little whore (she isn't even a serious actress, she's just famous for having fucked way too many famous actors like you, and you already know that, everyone knows that). And you said what, you want to offer me your money? I wouldn't take any of your money, even if I needed it to survive, you filthy son of a . . .

'Yes, of course. Why not?' I said.

I mean, I had been a fool for him so many times, it wouldn't really make a difference if I did it again, right? And, having them around maybe wouldn't be all that bad. Better than to be all alone in this blizzard, on Christmas Eve. At least I'd feel safer. That was pretty much the only reason I said yes.

'Oh Dolores, thank you so much. Really, we appreciate it so much!'

'Yeah, yeah. Listen, when will you be here?'

'Umm . . . At around eight, I think? We have to hurry up; they said there will be more wind and snow during the night; We have to make it to your place as soon as possible.'

That meant in around three hours. Oh, dear.

'Good! See you then!' I said quickly and hung up.

Oh dear, I thought and slapped my forehead. *What am I doing?*

III

I stood in front of the mirror in the hall, practicing a smile I was going to give to the guests once they arrived.

I wore a long, tight black and white dress, my favorite one—it looked really good on my tall, slender figure. My long, dark straight hair was tied in a slick, low ponytail. Just for the sake of this occasion, I went a bit further with my makeup than I usually would. Some black eyeshadow to match the color of my eyes, and red lipstick. I looked and felt amazing. *Let him see you shine, girl. Let him see what he lost.*

Damn, I couldn't believe I was still so bitter about this . . .

But the truth was, that's just how I always was. At this point, it wasn't about losing Peter anymore. Losing someone who did something so horrible to you isn't really losing, you know? More like dodging a big bullet. But there was something else. I was proud. *Really* proud. And if I ever stopped being mad about the fact that he even *dared* to leave someone like *me* and go with the stupid Tamara Nichols, then . . .

No, that's enough. You're only hurting yourself like this, I thought. *He doesn't seem bothered at all. He's happy, having a great time with his new fiancé.*

I remembered it being a really big deal back when it happened, when the rumours first started.

Of course, it was never fair. I worked so hard to get

where I was now, but it seemed that the thing I'd mostly be remembered by is that I was that girl who was dumped by the great irresistible ladies' man Peter Watts. Meanwhile, his career seemed just fine. *He's just so charming and romantic, he couldn't help it, he fell in love again and that was it . . . .*

Made me want to vomit.

Once again, I looked in the mirror. *Okay, looking good! Don't get discouraged now. It's just one night. You can do this.*

I went to the kitchen and prepared some nice wine glasses for the guests. We were going to have a good time, all right. I wanted to be as nice as could be, so he wouldn't have a single bad thing to pin on me, nothing nasty to talk about to his fiancé once they had gone away.

The blizzard outside seemed to have gotten even worse since the phone call. I wasn't even able to see clearly through the window, as it was now almost fully dark. Oh, wouldn't it be nice if our love birds got stuck in the snow somewhere and froze to death? I giggled. Okay, time to stop. The clock showed seven o'clock. One more hour.

IV

The bell rang. Quickly, I fixed my dress, took another look to make sure that my hair still looked fine. *All looking great. Let's do this.* Why was I so nervous?

I opened the door, and gave the guests the best grin I could possibly make. I most likely looked more creepy than welcoming. 'Come in,' I said. Peter even went as far to *shake hands* with me, and then Tamara did the same. The touch of her wet, cold little hand felt like touching a snake, and I may or may not have cringed at that moment. My face never lies, I thought. *I can be as nice and warm as possible, but that* face *doesn't lie.* Besides, I was there just to give them shelter for one night; it's not like I *had* to act

163

like I was delighted to see my ex-boyfriend with his new gal or anything, because we all knew that certainly wasn't true.

Funny thing is, Peter hadn't even changed that much. He looked a little bit older, but overall. . . . Why did I feel weak in the knees again? No. *No more of that, okay?*

But yes, he looked good; I couldn't deny it. After all, he was one of the most desirable actors of the period. His dark hair, grey eyes, and a big, kind of mischievous smile . . . and Tamara, she looked fine too, all right. She was younger than me, that was obvious—she was around twenty-three or so. A little shorter than me, red-haired and with a stupid smile, just the type of woman Peter needed. I must have accidentally slipped a smile there, because she smiled back at me, thinking that I was trying to be polite. *My ass,* I thought, and grinned again.

The evening went on pretty well, despite all the fake smiles at the beginning. We were sitting on the big leather sofa in front of the fireplace; I brought out some wine (fancy wine, because I'm not cheap), put some music on the record player, and did my best to be talkative and not show how goddamn cranky and hurt I was. Occasionally, I'd catch Peter looking at me.

The thing is, after some time, I started to feel better. The evening wasn't all that bad, not at all! Little by little, my bitterness went away, and I was finally able to relax and talk to them without sounding overly grumpy or sarcastic. Can you believe it? Even Peter seemed less pretentious and arrogant than he used to be when we were together. He was weirdly calm and pleasant. As for Tamara, I liked her too, dammit. She seemed way nicer in person than on TV. We talked about her new upcoming movie, a romantic comedy called *From Zero to Angel*— pretty offensive title, huh?—but overall, I felt happy for her. And who knows if those rumours about her sleeping with famous guys were true? She seemed a lot nicer than many 'modest' actresses I had met in the past. In fact, at that moment, I even thought we could, you know, be *friends.*

V

Surprisingly, Christmas Eve with my ex and his new fiancé, by that point, was actually a success. Toward the end of the night, I showed them to their room, after which Tamara went to take a bath. Peter and I stayed in the living room. Suddenly, there was this awkward silence between us.

Finally, I began talking.

'Hey, I never thought I'd admit this, you know me . . . .' I giggled, and continued, 'but I'm really happy for you. She seems great. And you, you look so happy, too. I'm sorry for being so rude at the beginning. Guess I was just too stressed out about spending Christmas Eve alone in my house, in the middle of the blizzard. And of course, I never expected your phone call! But I'm glad you came here, truly.' I smiled at him.

He relaxed a little. 'Thank you so much, Dee, I feel so relieved. It was so uncomfortable for me to dial your number, but I'm so thankful for your kindness. Who knows what would have happened if we . . . .'

He saw something, which interrupted him.

'Hey, is that . . . ?' he asked, pointing at the wall behind me.

On the wall, there was a small axe, not a very useful one for wood, (or at least I thought so; I never chopped wood myself, so I wasn't sure), which I had got from Peter as a present a long time ago.

And why the axe, you may wonder? Well, that axe was

165

kind of the reason we met. You see, ten years ago—the year was 1959—I was nineteen years old, and had just gotten my first big role in a teen romantic comedy called *The Lovesick Lumberjack.* You've guessed it, Peter was the lead actor in this one, playing the role of my romantic interest. The movie itself was as cringeworthy as can be, and yet, it became a success, mainly among younger audiences.

Instantly, I went back in time, and smiled a little painful smile. 1959 was a hard one. My parents died in early January that year, and, being an only child, I was suddenly on my own. My world fell apart. It wasn't until August that year that I was ready to accept a new role in a movie. The Lumberjack movie was, like I said, a success, and also the reason I became really famous. But it was, too, how I first met Peter. The movie had finished filming in late '59, and by that time, we were already madly in love. Peter was twenty-three at the time, and already quite well known for his good looks and sense of humour. After the movie premiered, I got to keep the axe as a reminder of my first big box office, and also of Peter.

I know it's pretty morbid to keep an axe as a decoration, but it was so special to me, and I couldn't throw it away, even after we broke up, which happened eight years after *The Lumberjack.*

'I can't believe you still have it! It's been such a long time.' He seemed amused now, and way more relaxed at last. He walked up to the wall and picked the little thing up. It looked a bit ridiculous in his big hands. It was never meant to be a real one, I believed, just an artifact for a silly teenage movie. Peter seemed to be so delighted by it now. But he soon put it away.

'It's time for bed.' He smiled again. I was standing close to him, my back to the wall. For a second, I had a flashback

he's grabbing you, pinning you to the wall, as he sticks his tongue in your mouth, and you reach for him, kissing him back, hungrily, running your fingers through his hair, as he's kissing your neck now and you're moaning and

I shook it off. That was once, but never again, no. I looked away, embarrassed, as if he could read my thoughts. Too much wine tonight? Maybe that was it. Maybe.

'Hey, Dee, is everything okay?' I hadn't seen Tamara come down the stairs.

'Yeah, I just . . . I feel a little drunk,' I smiled. 'Well, I better go lock the front door. And, if you need me, make sure to knock loudly because I need to lock my room too. I tend to sleepwalk, and I don't want to scare the two of you.' I looked up at Pete. 'You know I've been sleepwalking ever since. . .' And then I stopped. Why did I say that? Ever since my parents died, yes, and he knew about it. *Oh, it's definitely time to sleep.* I didn't want to louse this up even further.

VI

I slept rather restlessly. Around this time of the year, I'd always dream about the past Christmases which I had spent with my parents, and it would always make me sad. I had the same old dream tonight. I was a little girl, and there was just Mom, Dad, and me, so happy and careless. You see, both of my parents used to be actors, both big names, Mom in the theatre, Dad on the screen. Evelyn and Jonas Bates. I was pulled into this from an early age and soon wanted to become a successful actress myself. However, I didn't get my first big role until after my parents' unfortunate accident which took their lives only a year before my first big movie came out. At that point, it wasn't about fame or money anymore. I was sad because I never got to make them *really* proud, you know? That's something I never stopped being sad about. *I only wish Mom and Dad were here to see this*—that was my only thought each time I succeeded in my acting career.

This night in particular, I couldn't exactly fully remember the dream I had. I only know that I woke up in the middle of the night, after some strange sound coming from upstairs.

At first, I felt a little panicky, but then I remembered I wasn't alone. I heard the door creak, and after that, a couple of seconds of the bed springs creaking, before it got quiet again. I smiled at how silly I was. Probably one of them was just using the bathroom, or something like that.

I relaxed and went back to sleep . . .

. . . only to be awakened again, two hours later.

Something felt wrong. I got a sudden urge of fear, a strange sensation

he's standing at the foot of your bed. don't open your eyes. he's there, watching you. no, they are there, both of them. they are laughing at you, as you're

No. I finally opened my eyes. No one in the room. I listened closely. Be careful of those bed creaking sounds, I told myself. Because, if they have decided to fuck in *my* house, then . . . .

But I heard nothing.

I looked to the side and flinched a little when I saw it.

The door of the bedroom was ajar. I locked it before going to bed! I know I did, I. . . .

Or maybe I forgot? It was probably that. It was definitely more comforting than thinking that there was someone in the room with me, that one of them *broke* into my bedroom for god knows what reason.

I looked around again. No one was here. All clear. Was someone *trying* to . . . ? No. No. *You're making things up.* I got up, closed the door quietly, then turned the key. The moment my body touched the bed again, I realized just how tired I was. My whole body was aching, actually. Outside, the wind was making a wheezing sound. I shrugged a little, but after I got warm underneath the covers, I finally went into deep, peaceful sleep.

I failed to see the charred footprint next to my bed until it was too late.

VII

When I woke up, it was quite dark outside. I got up from the bed and went over to the window. The snow reached almost to one third of the downstairs windows, and the snowflakes never stopped falling. The weather forecast on the radio wasn't too optimistic either. Christmas morning. . . . I thought of Pete and Tamara. There's no way on earth they'd be reaching the Cot Castle anytime soon. In fact, I was already thinking of offering that they stay over for an extra day or two. My conscience wouldn't let me make them just go outside in the middle of all of this. Yes, I thought, I will definitely ask them to stay. We had a lovely time last night, and might as well try to deepen that friendship now. Besides, I felt happy for finally not being alone on Christmas.

I made some coffee and sat down in front of the TV. The time was passing quickly and, when I finally remembered to look at the clock, I realized it was almost 10 am. Why weren't Pete and Tamara getting up? It was a little strange. Yes, they were very tired from the trip, but I expected them to be up earlier. Oh well. *Maybe I should just let them rest instead.*

Another hour passed. *Should I go and check if everything is okay?* I wasn't hearing any sounds from the upstairs. At this point, I was getting concerned. If it hadn't been for

169

the blizzard, I would have suspected that maybe they left in the night. But they wouldn't be able to unlock the door; it didn't make any sense. Looking outside didn't help either, because I couldn't even see their car through all of the ice on the window. Something was off.

'Peter? Tamara! Are you two awake?' I yelled from downstairs. No answer.

I started up the stairs. My heart was beating really fast. *Why are you nervous?* I asked myself. *Maybe they're just asleep. Maybe . . . .*

The bedroom door was ajar. The blinds were still down. *They're probably still sleeping, they. . . .*

I opened the door, slowly. The light from the hall now shone into the bedroom. I froze.

The bedsheets, pillows, and the carpet on Tamara's side of the bed were all drenched with blood. At the sight, my legs turned into stone. I leaned forward, afraid of what I would see. She was lying on the bed, on her back, her skull split in half, her brains pouring out from the gaping hole, mixing with her long, red hair. I turned my back and vomited.

no no no no

Next to her was Peter, also lying on his back. His jaw was dangling from his face, attached only by the skin on his cheek on the right side. His eyes were open and still staring at the ceiling. I made another step forward, and suddenly backed away when I saw that I had stepped on something. I looked down. It was a severed hand. A man's hand. Next to it, I saw charred footprints, mixed with blood.

I ran from the room, out of breath, silent. Funny thing was, despite all of this, my mind still felt weirdly *calm*. My body was raging with fear and anxiety, but my mind. . . . Almost as if it was telling me that everything would be all right. It still couldn't fully grip that something so horrible happened. I was afraid. *Is whoever did this still in the house?* I *had* to remain calm, if I wanted to save my own life. I remembered the door of my own bedroom that had been ajar. Why didn't this person kill *me*?

The footprints. Follow the footprints. On the shaky legs, I dragged myself to the fireplace. Somehow, I didn't see that the axe had been missing from the wall the whole time. And then my eyes caught on something really strange. It was the fireplace. Among the charred remains of the wood, I noticed something white. Something like a rag? *I don't remember burning anything.*

I looked down at my clothes. I was quite drunk last night, but I was pretty sure I wasn't wearing *this* to bed. My current bed gown was red. I was almost entirely sure I had been wearing a white one. The one that was now laid burned inside of the fireplace.

I began to panic. *No. Please. It can't be, I would never. . .*

ohh you would, darling, and you did. You thought you would ever be over this? You know what you did. You got up, and you got that axe. You went into their room. Remember that Peter was trying to fight back? That's why you chopped his hand off. While he was busy bleeding out, you took care of Tamara, who was too shocked to even move. A piece of cake! What a stupid bitch. And then, you gave Pete one more big shove with the little axe, and he was gone too. You put them in the bed together, next to each other, just like the newlyweds that they'll never be. All thanks to you. You finally did what you were dreaming of ever since you heard about their engagement. Okay, maybe not like this, but your wish came true anyway. Now they will never end up married. Peter will never break your heart again, because, you know, he's dead!! You burned your bloody clothes in the fireplace to get rid of

I sat down on the floor, defeated. *Remember you used to do all kinds of things while sleepwalking? All kinds of forbidden things, especially. You knew this wasn't right, but the idea was*

171

there, buried in the back of your mind. You pushed it away. But you couldn't fight against it for very long. You can't fight against me, *and you know it.*

I looked down at my feet. There was still some char on them. Somehow, I failed to notice it all morning. I got it on my feet as I was getting the axe. The axe! My eyes went back to the fireplace. Remains of the melted axe head were buried among the ashes. I had tried to burn the weapon too.

VIII

Still sitting on the floor, I felt tears coming up my throat. My shallow breathing now turned into sobs. My insides were burning, and suddenly, I bent down, coughing, feeling the sudden urge to vomit. but nothing came out of my mouth. The realization hit me too hard. You'd think that there would be a limit to how much a human mind can endure, but there is none.

I knew I had to do *something*, but I didn't know what.

I got up, hurriedly. The bodies upstairs, I had to do something with the bodies.

One of my feet slipped as I was getting up. Somehow, I kept my balance.

My head was throbbing with pressure.

Again, creaking sounds came from upstairs, and I instantly froze.

it's them, they're coming for you they're

It was the wind.

I took another step, and, as my foot caught in a little pile of charcoal (it was everywhere), I slipped again.

Time suddenly slowed down, and I saw myself falling, toward the fireplace, neck first right onto the spikes of the little decorative gate in front of the firebox.

shouldn't have put it there

The voice in my head laughed.

at least you won't have to take care of the dead bodies now
haa haa . . .

The cold, sharp metal pierced through soft flesh

it's the payback . . .

and then I knew no more.

AUTHOR'S NOTE

The best ideas always come at the most random moments.

It was yet another boring evening in quarantine, sometime in 2020. I was stuck inside with my phone as my only company (not like I had a social life before the quarantine, but never mind). As often happens, I tend to go down various rabbit holes during these moments, especially *YouTube* rabbit holes. This time, however, I wanted to check a few songs I haven't heard since my childhood, just to see if I'll still like them. Somehow this one song popped into my head—it was *Cool* by Gwen Stefani. I used to adore that song when I was 9 or 10, although, as a non-native English speaker, I had no clue what the song was about.

Finally, I understood the lyrics.

And saw the music video for the first time, in which Gwen Stefani is visited by her ex and his new love. And that's when it 'clicked' inside of my head. What if we added an axe in there . . .

I can't say for certain exactly when this happened, but

I do remember that this submission call was open and that's why I thought of the winter setting. And, it proved to be a great combination. A year prior to this, I could never, even in my wildest dreams, imagine myself even writing, let alone being published. Writing was something I had done as a teen, but abandoned after the 'grownup' routine came into my life. But then 2020 came, I got to know Jay Alexander and many other names from the indie community, and, after trying my luck briefly with two-sentence horror stories, my first 'real' story, "The Letter", came to life. And then many others.

Including "The Christmas Eve", of course.

Carmilla Yugov

REALMER, REDEEMER

JOE CLEMENTS

REALMER, REDEEMER
BY JOE CLEMENTS

Hell is a personal thing, I know that now. There are no fire-laden valleys or skeletal boatmen traversing magma lakes, at least not in my experience. These things however may well be for some, dependant on themselves and, as I've recently discovered, the particular way in which they die.

My death, or should I say my first death, was brief according to outside sources. It didn't feel that way. It felt as though time didn't exist at all in that place; by the time I was resuscitated innumerable lifetimes of the purest suffering had passed through my perspective filter.

Whether a real born from my psyche or birthed from some higher judgement this place—if it is indeed a place—should not be found through any conscious human effort. The aeons of obscure trepidation felt within are reserved for those feeling and I believe wholeheartedly that most, if not all, who are subject to such horror never again see the light of day. A light I have not yet seen myself as I write by that of a candle amidst a peculiar clarity which sat me straight in my hospital bed this night. Each sleeping nightmare puts me right back there, each projected face the same as that which hunted me within those wretched corridors. The falling snow beyond these thinly-paned windows brings me, ever momentarily, the stillness to recollect, to record and preserve and externalise my horror so that I might not suffer alone in the mere knowledge of it.

'Hang here,' he said to me, 'I need to make a quick drop off,' as he pulled his Fiat Punto alongside a farm-track entrance. I had three jackets fastened around me and was still too cold to bother wondering why he could he dealing so far out in the sticks. He locked the doors, probably through force of habit, before disappearing into the night. I might have shouted were it not for the shivering. If I'd known then half of what I know now . . . I don't know. Perhaps it would be different. I rubbed my hands for a time but quickly tired of it. By the time I began to worry, my fingers were too cold to pry the little lock-nub from the door. The old Punto's electronics showed no signs of life. I remember sitting and hoping, convincing myself he would emerge from the colourless landscape at any moment.

I'm sure you'll have heard somewhere that when close to death your life flashes before your eyes. For me it was less a flash, and less my life than a series of disappointments, embarrassments and deep regrets. As they began to flood in I tried forcing the door with my shoulder, knowing it, on a level, to be futile. I was far too weak. I'd already chosen my fate by remaining indolent when all the warning signs were there.

It is also commonly said that one might experience a dark tunnel with a blinding light at one end. To such a vision I was subjected, but that light, deceptively so, was not the end at all, but simply another tunnel. Lighter, yes, but a tunnel nonetheless. Looking behind me I saw no entrance to have come through, merely another extension of the same, grey corridor. It was about wide enough to fit the Punto down, but not a lot else. Upward it stretched to about twice my height, its walls decorated with incomprehensible symbols representing some ancient language. Some looked like Egyptian hieroglyphics but depicting far stranger, far older meanings. The whole place had an air of long-forgotten mystery, seemingly built on ideals and concepts since bred out of the human race through millions of evolutionary years. Within these shapes were those of eyes, embedded in their forms as if drawn in to be hidden, yet now that I noticed them they appeared everywhere as stars would to one's night-adjusting eyes. All bared down in silent judgement.

I have already spoken of a pursuer in these halls, and now was around the time I first heard it; that growl like lightning tearing boulders from a mountaintop, the hissing like a gas-line exploding into the eardrums. The sounds were from afar, yet the beast was close as told by the words I could hear it utter, words that sounded like roaring flames and nothing more. Redeemer was the name it insisted upon, though I knew it to be *Realmer*.

Another crack around a hundred metres ahead and the wall crumbled inwards there. In it stepped; cloven hoof hissing on the snow that seemingly fell from nowhere and lay thick on the stone, curling, malformed horns scraping and grinding against the carven limestone ceiling. Warped into these horns were great antlers as if the beast could not decide which to grow, leaving it with a doubly threatening crown of twisted bone. Its hoof rose again to reveal a circle of ice where the hoof had frozen the ground ever further. I smelled it, the permeating odour of decay that hung on the cold, still air.

I've read about Minotaurs in mythology, great half-man-half-bull creatures. The Realmer was similar, though what of a Minotaur would be bull was here stag. The dead-yet-frantic eyes and stretched mouth gave the impression of a reanimated head from some hunter's wall. It looked blindly but I knew it saw me. Its shoulders were fur-lined as an expensive winter coat, yet most of it was hairless, from its torso of oversized, disproportioned muscle pulled over a winding skeleton to its steeple phallus which gestured at me as its next victim. Jet stone teeth snapped twixt a lipless jaw.

I had seen enough. Shoes skidding on the snow, I ran. I felt its pursuit, felt the gap between us growing rapidly smaller. Its footsteps shook frost from the wall's illustrations which, as I ran, morphed and flickered like a demented zoetrope into antediluvian hieroglyphics depicting generations of misanthropic, time-lost savagery at the Realmer's behest. The stories, though ancient and distant, seemed somehow familiar; nothing I'd ever heard or been taught but each beginning, middle and end I passed washed over me like tides of hyper-vivid déjà vu. Still it gained on me.

I remember thinking that this must be what it's like to watch a bullet soaring towards you, slowed to a thousandth its speed by deaths-verge perspective, fixed into a contemplative inevitability while death slowly, unrelentingly approaches.

The walls watched me mockingly as I turned another corner, skidding on the icy stone. Somewhere in my subconscious a voice was asking why. *Why me? Whatever did I do to deserve such torment? If this is Hell, what are my sins? I've always tread lightly, never made a wave big enough to hurt a soul. What then are my sins?*

Silence ensued before the Realmer appeared around the next corner. I turned tail and returned as I had come, slipping on his iced over footprints, wholly surprised he had not caught me yet. I could have been running for seconds or days. Fear and panic converged in a pathetically emotional maelstrom. I sobbed and ran, a wretch in the hands of inescapable evil. The corridor changed; a dead end, no, a corner! I took it only to be faced with him again. I saw him like I'd seen nothing before or since, so aware of his terrible energy that my legs now failed me. A screaming gale from beyond shook him none, only whipping at the steam rising from his impossible form. The walls watched us, locked in our seemingly endless staring contest. He stood as some hideous ode to every broken man's idea of masculinity, his head suddenly every hunter's needless, ego-driving kill, it's body a version of my own watered-down, dysmorphic self-image. The eyes on the wall were laughing now, laughing in the scornful voices of every opposing party, every contradicting naysayer I allowed impede on my self-worth.

Another gale, the wind of a talker who will never listen for fear of what he may hear. Cold as the words he threw at all those who would humour him, love him, cold enough to never melt at the affection of another. 'What are my sins?' The beast's smouldering tongue spoke. 'I never hurt anyone.'

And I knew my sins in their entirety as it gored my tender form, my stomach but a film packaging to be punctured for the meat within to be wholly feasted upon. It gored and devoured, minced and ground and tore within those frozen halls until the aeons of man had long past, the physical realm crumbled before me and all that was left was suffering.

EVERY HUNT IS A COLD ONE

MARCUS HAWKE

EVERY HUNT
IS A COLD ONE
BY MARCUS HAWKE

White.

Endless, blinding white as far as the eye could see. Hope was sick of it. No, sick wasn't right. Sick didn't even begin to do justice to the hatred she had for it. And the feeling was mutual.

Darkness was easy. It could be honed, hidden in, used to her advantage. All she had to do was stay still and silent, and it would welcome her like an old friend. But up here everything was exposed. Each breath showed in plumes of ghostly mist. Every step crunched in the snow, telling anyone and anything within earshot where she was. Up here there was nowhere to hide.

And it was cold. Nothing new, of course. It was always cold now, everywhere. She could barely even remember a time before the Freeze now. So long ago it seemed more like a story Daddy had read her. Most of what she knew had come from him. But somewhere deep in the frozen recesses of her memory she recalled something other than white, and black, and the occasional red of blood. A time when winter was just one of the seasons. Of greens and blues. Sun and water. Other things she absolutely took for granted like wheat fields and pavement. They were still there of course. Just buried under tons of snow.

She couldn't think about that now. If she started, she'd never stop.

And the hunt was on.

The tracks led East, toward the City. She knew it was called Calgary, or had been once, but to her it was just the City'. Daddy said never to go to the City, but today she didn't have a choice. She and Adam hadn't eaten in days, and even if she caught something the meat couldn't always be trusted. And even if it could, it would barely be enough to go around.

Everything was running out. Food, water, wood. Time. They had gas up until a short while ago, enough to light the lamps at least. Now everything was scarce. Most of it for good, like ammo. There would never be more of that unless she was lucky enough to find some. Every tree nearby was either cut down, frozen solid, or buried under snow long ago, so most of the time having a fire was impossible. Only if she decided to burn that which she needed to survive. Or could not bear to see go up in flames. Oh, what she would give to feel one right now. Water wasn't a problem, but even in the shelter it couldn't always be melted enough to drink.

Everything ached. She hadn't eaten in days and her

bones showed through her skin. And Adam, he didn't look well. Weak and feverish when last she saw him. That was two days ago. She could hardly bear being away for so long but had been needing to venture further and further from home to catch anything at all for a while now.

This world was something no boy of six should have to face. He was her only saving grace, but sometimes she was sorry for bringing him into it. He had never even left the shelter.

Wind howled against her, biting through every crease and crack it could find. Though she was covered from head to toe, bound up in thick white layers like a mummy, it still got through. It always got through. The tracks were at risk of disappearing before her, but fortunately they were deep enough to last for a bit at least. Her own steps left very little trace thanks to a trusty pair of snowshoes fashioned out of a pair of tennis rackets. Daddy said they were used in a game 'pencil neck candy asses' used to play.

An hour passed.

Then two, during which she lost feeling from the waste down. Not completely, just enough to feel frostbite setting in.

Well into the third hour she found herself at the City limits. It appeared all of a sudden out of the blowing snow, looming before her like a ghost. The deer had gone right into it, its hoofprints now round and hard. Fresh.

As she crossed a bridge over the river, Hope took the bow from around her torso and fit it with an arrow. Her hand briefly fell to her side, patting the ice pick that dangled there clipped to her belt, telling her *I'm here if you need me.*

Signs, street lamps, streetlights, whole buildings, all encrusted with snow and ice. She kept her head low, just beneath the drifts lining each side of the street. They had been cars once. Now little more than dead machines. Useless as the corpses inside them. There were a number of things to watch for, and her prey was just one of them.

Amazing to think any animals could have survived in this at all, let alone for so long.

As she followed the deer tracks, she spied another set. Long and flat. A rabbit. Not a very big one and they went in the other direction, but something to eat was not to be passed up.

They grew fresher and fresher as she followed them down a side street. This, added with the wind easing up for the first time in days, reduced to a frigid breeze, made her job far easier.

And then she spotted it. So still it was nearly invisible, had it not been for that single wide leporine eye looking her way from the side beneath long ears. Wondering if she saw. It just sat there twitching its distinctly non-bloodied nose. Didn't appear to be sick.

Slowly, she raised the bow. Not enough to aim yet, just enough to size things up. To declare the intent to herself.

The rabbit crouched, making itself small.

She stopped moving. If it ran she would have to be

quick.

It remained still.

Her muscles flexed just enough to move the bow up again, while her other hand, or at least two fingers of it, began tensing the arrow against the bowstring.

A massive white paw swiped out at the rabbit from between two drifts. It ran away in a flash while Hope froze, inside and out.

Out stepped a mountain of a monster. The biggest bear Hope had ever seen in her life. There hadn't been many times, and they had all been from afar. And always with Daddy there, ready with his shotgun. He said that before the Freeze they used to live way further up North. How something so big made so little sound was a mystery. Despite its size, the bear was sickly. Thin. Weak and hungry. His bones showed through the patchy white fur that was pink in some places from having fallen out. Huffing out one hard, laboured breath after another through jagged teeth. The skin around one eye hung loose in the socket, and the eyeball along with it. And there, wetting the nose, was a stain of red. The snout dripped with it.

Clear signs of the Cold. Probably from eating too many that had caught it.

The bear turned and looked right at her.

His growl sounded desperate and weak, but still enough to send her running without a second thought. Hunter had become prey.

Nothing but the sound of massive footfalls, punishing the snow beneath it with every step, followed by the forced huff of each hungry breath.

Hitting him with an arrow — *if* she hit him — wouldn't even slow him down, only piss him off. Outrunning him became less and less of a possibility with every inch he gained on her.

But size wasn't everything.

She took a hard left down an alley, between two buildings. Skidding across the snow, digging a deep scar into it. The bear was fast. Heavy. Determined. Luckily though, he couldn't pivot worth a damn, coming almost to a complete stop in order to follow.

She got a good thirty feet ahead, but the alley was long and solid with nowhere to turn. When he charged after her again, he meant it. She felt the impact of his weight in the frozen ground.

This may have been a bad idea.

The end was in sight, the narrow white around her ready to open back up into a blinding one the nearer she got to it.

A blast of hot breath hit her. The first warm thing she had felt in days. At least it would be the last thing she would remember.

A gunshot.

She hadn't heard one for years and stopped in her tracks. So loud even the bear halted.

Another tore through the air, pinging off the wall

behind her. She hit the deck and the bear continued forward, trying to squeeze out of the narrow alley.

Then came a third shot. The bear hit the ground. The last of the air escaping his lungs a prelude to the unnerving, unyielding silence that followed.

Hope knew all kinds of silences. There was the silence of the City, lacking not only sound, but life. The gentle one that falls over the entire world when it snows on Christmas morning. The harsh one which tethers the absence of affection between two people. The type that passed between her and Adam when they had nothing to talk about, which was often. Or just a lack of sound, pure and simple. But this was no common silence.

A frigid breeze blew through the City bringing with it a different kind of chill altogether, overtaking the one she felt in her body. Nowhere near so hard as before, diminished to a nosy whisper. Her perforated breath, forced out between chattering teeth as she shifted gears down from full throttle to idle, hacked and stalled until it finally produced a sound.

'H-hello?'

No response. Just the wind biting through every thin fold of her clothing, telling her to leave. This was a silence she had never known before. Deliberate. Irksome. The guilty quiet of someone who was there but chose not to speak.

She lifted one foot to start moving away.

Another shot rang out. Instantaneously, the ground

193

where her step would have fallen exploded in a pop of snow.

For a second—just a *second*—she had caught a flash come from somewhere in the murky white distance. The message was clear.

Don't Move!

Her heart raced and pumped ice water through her veins.

Then she heard something.

Crunch … crunch … crunch … crunch …

Hushed. Almost languid. Each *crunch* grew just a little louder. Closer.

She ditched the makeshift snowshoes and made a dash for it, the crunch of her own footsteps interrupted those that approached until she couldn't hear them. Any second she expected them to be ceased by a final shot, the world of white gone replaced by one of darkness forever.

The cover of what had once been an underground parkade came into view on the other side of the road. Nearly swallowed by drift after drift, but accessible. She ducked between snow-covered cars and slid smoothly down a hill.

Another shot. It missed, hitting the ground right next to her.

She didn't stop to look back as she made for cover. Couldn't afford to. From somewhere behind came the series of metal clicks of a reload.

Almost there. So near that the shadows touched her covered face now.

The next shot she felt as well as heard, screaming its ugly red pain into her foot just below the ankle, falling to one knee as she reached the shelter of darkness.

No time for pain, she thought, ducking behind a concrete pillar for cover.

Crunch . . . crunch . . . crunch . . . crunch . . .

She didn't even have time to appreciate being out of the endless wind and snow for the first time since leaving home, howling away just on the other side of the pillar like the churn of a violent sea.

Her hand fell to the ice pick again. It wasn't there.

Hope fit the bow with another arrow, having lost the first one somewhere during the chase.

Anything center mass was going to be protected by thick layers of padding. No good.

Same with the legs and a wound there wouldn't prevent him from firing.

A headshot would do it, but it's harder to hit.

Crunch . . . crunch . . . crunch . . . crunch . . .

With a long sharp breath, Hope steadied herself and made a move.

The shot came right away. She didn't even have time to aim, let alone fire . . . but then she hadn't meant to. Let him waste his shot. And then came the sound she was waiting for, the metallic clicks of a reload.

Everything moved in slow motion. She took aim, getting her first real view of the hunter. About thirty yards away. Red coat. Face covered by a ski mask and goggles. Holding a rifle which was half a second away from becoming dangerous again.

She fired. It missed completely, carried off by the wind and disappeared into the white. She took shelter behind the pillar and drew another arrow.

Four left.

The next shot hit the other side of the pillar.

Gotta make the next one count.

Crunch . . . crunch . . . crunch . . . crunch . . .

Much faster this time.

She bolted from behind the pillar, leaving a trail of bloody footsteps behind her. Stumbled and fell onto her back while trying to shoot the arrow at him as he rushed her.

All this for a rabbit, she thought as the butt of the rifle came down hard right in the middle of her forehead, robbing her of the partial dark and replacing it with a complete one.

Daddy was strict but nice. He taught her how to plough and sow the field. He taught her how to fish. How to drive the tractor. How to shoot, how to hunt, how to dress and clean a kill.

Daddy made her read scripture. Every day. No excuses. When she was finished, she'd start again. Daddy said the world was going all to Hell thanks to the rosary-rattlers, the heathen liberals, the Jews, the Muslims, and the queers. Well, he was right about things going to Hell at least. Only this Hell had frozen over. They didn't have a TV, but Daddy kept a radio for emergencies. The voices said that the ice caps had melted and released diseases trapped for millions of years.

Then one day, the radio voices stopped. Then there was only one country. One land. It's flag was white, but it didn't surrender.

Daddy said: 'We done fucked this world up so bad it's fuckin' us back.' He said that the End Times had come with ice rather than fire. That reminded her of a poem by Robert Frost that she had read in the school library:

Some say the world will end in fire,
Some say in ice.
From what I've tasted of desire
I hold with those who favor fire.
But if it had to perish twice,
I think I know enough of hate
To say that for destruction ice
Is also great
And would suffice.

Daddy made her do things. Not for himself, never for himself, but to replenish the earth. It said so right in the Book of Genesis when Lot had lain with his daughters. There was never any joy in it for him. He was just doing right by God. She wasn't sure she believed him, but she didn't hate him. Could never hate him. After all, he gave her Adam. And together, no matter how cold the world had become, they were a family.

Daddy went out hunting one day. Six years ago. And since then, he was gone.

When Hope woke, it was to the feel of something she hadn't known in so long that she had nearly forgotten it: warmth. The crackle of a fire came from behind her, heating the backs of her arms and neck. So nice, such a relief she could have cried. The wind was gone now, diminished from its constant howl to a distant whisper somewhere off to her right. Even more distant now that it was behind the soft guitar notes of a bossa nova tune trickling through the room. Refined and alien to her even before the Freeze.

Everything was numb. A sensation she had grown familiar with thanks to frequent sub-zero temperatures and frostbite. This was different though. Barely any feeling at all from the waist down, and she couldn't feel her left leg at all. Probably a good thing considering that was the foot that had been shot, but the rest would almost certainly be blistered and black this time. Might even lose a toe.

Her cheeks, the bridge of her nose, anywhere the wind could slip through burned. Oh, the tragic irony in the fact that cold could burn, reminding her of that poem again.

The fireplace cast a shadow play against the surfaces of everything in front of her, the dim orange glow now keeping the odious blue dark of night at bay. Her vision was blurry to a point of near invisibility but she could just make out candles on a table. Others sat around it, not moving but looking her way.

Her head throbbed with a dull but persistent pain throughout her head. It would have been far worse had it not been for the drugs pumping through her bloodstream. She smelled clean, soap mixed with a vague but unmistakable antiseptic smell of iodine. Liquid water being a tough enough thing to get in the first place, she hadn't had the luxury of a bath in a long time.

For a moment she thought everything might be ok. She flexed her muscles, meaning to reach up and rub the haze from her eyes, only to find her arms strapped down to those of the chair she was in. A belt around her midsection held her tight to the back of it.

Footsteps approached. Same pace as before only minus the crunch of snow, replaced by the jingling of keys.

'Ah, you're awake,' came a slightly nasal voice just beyond the cloud of her vision. He placed something in the middle of the table—her nostrils were filled with the savoury smell of cooked meat, garlic, and rosemary—came around the table past one of the other guests (who still hadn't moved or spoken since she regained consciousness) and knelt down next to her. Bearded and balding. A bit sickly as though his face had once been fuller. Nothing much to look at aside from his kind brown eyes. It all felt shallow though. Thin ice in April.

'What's your name?'

'Hope,' she answered with little breath.

'Hope,' he echoed, soothed by the very sound of it. 'Perfect.' His hands went to her face. Roughened and calloused from years of being forced to use them, but like his face it was only on the surface. The palms still held some semblance of their former refinement. They had once been treated, cared for. Precise. Vapor trails streamed out from the candles as he guided her head upward, tickling her face from the slight tremor that shook his fingers. A thumb pulled down the bottom lid of one eye and then the other. 'How are you feeling?'

'Dizzy,' she said.

'Hmm, you will for a little while but the anaesthetic should be wearing off soon.' He stood, rattling the keyring clipped to his belt, and went around to the other end of the table. 'Well I hope you're hungry because we've got a proper feast tonight.'

'Feast?' The word felt foreign on her lips.

'Oh yes. It's not everyday we have a guest for dinner, is it kids? But where are my manners? I'm Murray, and this is my family. Well . . . '

Her vision cleared up. Sitting on either side of a long dinner table sat two bodies—a boy of about ten and a girl about eight. Dressed, groomed, a full set of cutlery set out before them. White plastic bags covered their heads, taped at the neck with blood smeared where the noses would be. Smiley faces were drawn on them in thick black felt marker.

'I guess it's our family now.' The smile on his face was all too real. 'Kids, say hello to Hope. Your new mother.'

She tried to flex, test the strength of leather straps holding her in place, praying for any sign of weakness in them. This time her movement sent a tube connected to her hand swaying. It was connected to an IV suspended above her from a stainless steel stand next to her. She followed it down to the floor and saw that the chair she was in had wheels on it. Some of the feeling returned to her legs . . . to one of them at least.

'Oh god,' she said, looking at the steaming dish on the table, 'Where did that meat come from?' Hope nudged herself away from the table and looked beneath. She saw only one leg. With her entire body and soul, she screamed. In pain. In sorrow. In hopes that someone would hear and come to help. But there was no one.

'I understand that you're upset,' said Murray, 'But it needed to be amputated and . . . well . . . waste not.' He cut himself off a piece with his fork and knife and began to chew. 'Not bad, actually. Anyway, you won't need it here. I'll take good care of you. I promise.'

Maybe he was right. Maybe this wasn't so bad. *I'm tired of hunting, tired of fighting, tired of the cold. But . . .*

'My boy . . . '

'What boy?'

'I have a son. He's out there, alone. Has been for days.'

Murray stood from his seat. 'Good god! Why didn't you say so?'

Must have slipped my mind, asshole.

'Did you hear that, kids? You're getting a new brother too. Where is he?'

'North . . . north-wes—' Her head fell forward and hung.

Chair legs squealed across the floor followed by the same hurried footsteps as before. Hands trembling, he lifted her head up, thinking she had fainted. As soon as she caught a glimpse of his face close to hers, she lunged.

Hope bit into the freshly shaved skin of his neck. He jerked away but she held on for dear life with every tiny dagger in her mouth. They both collapsed to the floor, toppling both the wheelchair and the IV pole over. She fell on top of him, ripping and tearing back and forth until the jugular broke and the initial gush of blood became a torrent.

His hands flew to his neck as he tried to stop the leak, wailing as he climbed frantically to his feet. He rushed back to the other side of the table, grabbed a cloth napkin up, and pressed it against the wound.

'Why would you do that? Huh?! Why—' The cloth of the napkin had turned from white to red in no time. 'Oh god.'

He hurried down the hall and disappeared. Assuming Murray could stop the bleeding, Hope figured she had two minutes before he returned.

Hope spat what blood she had in her mouth onto the floor, careful not to swallow any. It was the first warm thing she had had in her mouth in a long time. She didn't even mind the taste. And she was so hungry.

No. Not now. You went this long without resorting to that. Now is not the time.

Still strapped to the wheelchair, she wriggled herself over to the blood she had spat, and tried to get as much of it as she could on her hands.

Not enough.

From the bathroom down the hall, all she heard was things slamming and his wailing in pain and fear for his life as it poured out of him.

She wriggled further to the trail of blood he'd left behind him, expecting any moment he might return, neck bandaged, towering over her, with something blunt and nasty to pound what was left of her to death.

Hand sufficiently wet now (thankful for the small blessing of not having to look at it) Hope twisted her wrist against the leather strap and freed herself of it. With one bond gone, the other was no problem, nor was the belt around her waist.

She grabbed a knife from the table and crawled on her elbows beneath it. Hunched and waiting for him to reappear.

'C'mon,' she fumed. 'C'mon you fucker.' Every second he didn't show, the more she felt it coming. 'Come on!'

No more sound came from the bathroom. Eventually she realized that it was going to stay that way, and was lost to quiet sobs.

Can't I just lay here by the fire? she thought. *That's all I want. Warmth and heat. A world of lovely golden light and no more of the cold.* And lay there she did, allowing herself a few precious moments of this small pleasure. It stretched out into the longest, most unbearable sigh. Cruel really, because it could not last.

Hope crawled out from under the table, flipped the wheelchair back upright, and — after a few failed attempts — hoisted herself into it.

Carefully, slowly, she wheeled herself down the hall.

He could still be alive. She knew that. He could be crouched, quietly waiting for her to come to him. But she needed those keys. Without them, the journey back home would be impossible now.

Not a sound from the other side of the door. Cautiously she pushed it open with the knife. A quick peek inside before ducking back around the doorjamb.

No movement. No breath.

She looked again and took in the few details she could see properly.

White and black tiles laid out in a checked pattern on the floor. Walls painted in a smooth eggshell. Countertops of hard mottled marble. And a real porcelain clawfoot tub at the far end.

Everything in here bled, marred by smears and spatters of blood. It streaked over the rim of the bathtub where a single leg stuck out over the side. Dripped off a hand that stood up in the air, its fingers twitching.

Funny how this tiny show of movement confirmed his demise more than absolute stillness. Even so, she approached ready for anything. Clutching the knife so hard it hurt.

There he lay, drenched and red and lifeless. Eyes still open, the expression on his face vacant. Looking for something he would never see. His other hand rested on his thigh, holding a surgical needle fit with stitching. Too little too late.

He couldn't harm her now. He was no longer the hunter. Just another dead thing. Still there was an eerily tragic way about him. A man looking for company, driven mad by loneliness, despair, solitude, and loss. Ceased to be.

She thought about crawling into his arms. Now while he was still warm. Just to feel it once more. An embrace. The feel of being in someone's arms again. Even an enemy. Even a corpse. To know it was real once again and always had been.

At least, that was how she saw him. It was a lot better than he deserved.

Hope unclipped the keys from his belt. He moved in her mind, but nowhere else as she wheeled herself out the door, leaving him truly and finally alone.

*

Back at the farm. Amazing she still saw it that way, even after all this time. It was little more than a frozen, broken-down husk of what had once been. The house was gone completely. Only the barn remained and it was badly in need of repair. But it would always be where she fed chickens. Where she played and swam. Learned how to plant. How to grow. How to shoot. How to survive.

Using the rifle as a crutch, she awkwardly got out of Murray's truck. Some silly part of her thought maybe, just maybe, the wind would relent just this once. But no. It bit into every haphazardly covered part of her all the same.

She made her way into the barn. The roof was full of holes that had fallen in with the weight of snow and ice, snowflakes swirling down from above, and the rest looked like it could go anytime now.

Thankfully not much snow had covered the trap door to the shelter since she left, and clearing it away would not have been easy standing on one leg. She gave the handle one unsteady tug and nearly lost her balance. The second time it was flung open.

'Adam?' she called. 'Adam, come quick. Mama needs your help.'

It was true. Not just to get into the shelter, but to get back to the penthouse, to get whatever food, provisions, and supplies they could from it. She had kept him safe and sound up to this point, but with everything she would need his help from now on. Far too much to ask of a boy of six, but now there was no choice.

No response from inside.

She began to hop down the stairs, bracing herself on her elbow along the railing. The rifle crutch missed the step it was supposed to land on and she fell. Only a few steps, but now every inch of her hurt.

On her side she craned her neck upward and saw him sitting with his back to her not far way. Still covered by the blanket she had wrapped around him herself, staring at a wood burning stove of nothing but cold ashes.

'Adam,' she choked out. Still no response.

Hope crawled over to a nearby chair covered with clothes and blankets she had found elsewhere and hobbled over to where he was.

At first she thought he might still be alive and tried to shake him awake. But there was no color left in his face. She couldn't even bear to say his name again.

Hope took him in her arms and wept. Her boy. Her son. All she had left, now also claimed by the cold. She rocked him back and forth, held tight against her breast. He was still warm . . . and she was so hungry.

So hungry.

AUTHOR'S NOTE

This story came from a very weird place. It was during a time when everyone was stuck in their homes like a bunch of hermits, afraid of a virus that seemed to be everywhere, during a time of the year I loathe, with all manner of personal issues escalating from nuisance to calamity. And all on top of countless other ongoing real world horrors, and while publishing my first novel, and . . . and . . . and . . . ..you get the idea.

I always hope for the best, of course. And that was how I originally planned to end this bleak little tale. But experience has far too often told me a different story. One where hope can be as hard to find as grass in winter. Don't get me wrong, I don't mean to sound pessimistic or anything—well, maybe a little—all I'm saying is that there's a reason why, in addition to hoping for the best, we also plan for the worst.

That's where this story came from. The worst place imaginable.

Enjoy!

Marcus Hawke

THE
VIOLENT SNOW
PATRICK WHITEHURST

THE VIOLENT SNOW
BY PATRICK WHITEHURST

Ray Jones could nap the day away, anytime, anywhere.

Since arriving at Number Twelve Pine Lane he'd done nothing but nap. Time to get up and get something unpacked. He had three days and he'd already wasted two hours passed out on the gold loveseat facing the fireplace like a swollen corpse. Originally smooth, the crushed velvet fabric these days felt more like a concrete driveway.

Sitting up, Ray fixed the collar of his threadbare, red flannel shirt and reached for the stretchy skinny jeans he'd tossed to the floor. A heavy, grey storm swallowed up most of the light from the day. He could see nothing through the window but blowing snow. If this whiteout kept up, those three days might be just the beginning. He'd thought he'd hear birds, the sound of a jeep or two, or a neighbour's distant chainsaw, but the storm ate all noise. The silence of a snowstorm became deafening in its nothingness.

Speaking to the empty fireplace, he struggled to hoist his jeans over his corpulent belly. 'Better get some warmth in this old cabin. Drink some damn coffee next.'

Yawning, he strolled over to the pile of dusty pine wood

stacked to the side of a shadowy stone hearth. His bare feet shuffled lazily over the plank floors. His cell phone vibrated in his pocket. Either the battery died or somehow a signal got through. He made no effort to check.

Number Twelve Pine Lane sat on a forty-acre parcel north of Flagstaff. Ray still hadn't explored all of it. He'd gotten to know the back porch quite well, having grilled and sat in the hot tub for the last few solitary vacations, which he called "hermications". The compact, two-story cabin featured a living room, kitchen, and downstairs bathroom. A cavernous bedroom and half-bath made up the second floor. Perfect for a guy working on his great American novel, or a guy that *told* people he was so he could get some peace. Between that and perfecting the two-hour nap, he wanted for nothing.

Snow flurries danced in ever-greying patterns on the other side of the window. Beyond he saw darkening nothingness, maybe the black outline of a pine tree here and there. They covered the property, leaving it in perpetual shade, and he adored it. Someday, maybe after the kids moved out, he'd ask Agatha to give up the four-bedroom place. She loved her oppressive Phoenix heat, untouchable cactus, and sour sweat. He preferred the higher altitudes of northern Arizona.

His breath fogged the icy window. 'She'd hate this.'

Ten minutes later, he flipped on a pot of coffee in the tight kitchen. A small fire burned in the living room hearth, casting black and orange shadows on the loveseat.

At the counter he went through the battle-scarred backpack he'd stuffed with crap to keep him busy. Three pairs of jeans, three flannels, three white boxers, and three rolls of white tube socks. He yanked out his creased 1975 Berkeley paperback of Frank Herbert's *Dune* and placed it next to the coffee maker. Nothing better than reading about hot sand in a snowstorm. He scratched the white stubble on his chin. Next to the backpack sat two bags of healthy groceries and his 2011 Dell laptop. A couple packages peeked from the top of one bag. Mail his wife had stuffed there. As if he planned to ponder bills. With the smell of steam-burned coffee filling his nostrils, he picked up the first package.

Postmarked from his buddy at Northern Arizona University. And it wasn't just a letter. Ray could feel something inside, misshapen and a bit heavy. A gift?

Intrigued, he tore into the parcel, finding an oddly-shaped, solid blue object. Looked like a gas mask with a hose attached to the bottom. Thing was big enough to stick on a ventriloquist dummy, but not quite big enough for his own face. *What the hell is this thing?*

A Post-It note hung from the flat side of the blue, bony-looking gadget. A brown splash stained the bottom of the bright yellow paper. Ray squinted to read the messy writing.

Dude, not supposed to do this . . . printed some extra 3-D copies of this unknown larynx. The specimen was found in an ice cave on the San Francisco Peaks, but we can't ID it. Some kind of animal fossil? Even Susan in Zoology hasn't pegged it. Weird, right? Anyway, thought you'd like some inspiration for your hermication while you pretend to write. One of a kind shit!—Chuck.

Chuck. *One of a kind* best bud.

Ray turned the object over in his hand. The hell was he supposed to do with the damn thing? The deafening snow was all but forgotten. Inside the electric-blue mask, he saw what looked like a flat tongue with a hole in the centre. It led down the inside of the tube, or maybe he should call it an *oesophagus,* albeit a 3-D printed *copy* of one. He set the thing on the counter and went for his cup of coffee. He'd kept a few dishes there. Made life easier than trucking a bunch of clanking porcelain up from the valley.

Behind him, an angry gust rattled the kitchen window, giving him a start. The glass shook in the frame. He smiled as much as he ever did, relieved to hear something outside. Better than silence. Filling a black mug, he felt his phone vibrate again. Rather than fish it out, his hand went to the face mask.

What the hell kind of animal did this belong to?

A Zoo Lab should know them all, right? Sounded like NAU had a mystery on their hands. Ray took a sip from the piping hot coffee. The bitterness burned a trail down his own oesophagus. The gift reminded him of a story he'd read in The NY Times some months ago about an Egyptian priest. He turned the noisy paper to read closely, the smell of ink in his nostrils. Nesyamun may have originated in

Thebes, but according to the article, his mummy ended up in the hands of researchers. That's when science turned blasphemous. These folks made a model of his throat and mouth and actually used it to generate sound, effectively making Nesyamun speak again.

After a few more piping hot sips he set the coffee on the counter. The larynx replaced it in his hands. Had they tried that over at NAU? Smart folks for sure, but had they made the throat speak? Ray put the model to his lips and inhaled. It smelled of plastic, like a freshly-opened Barbie doll for his daughter. Maybe the sound would be recognizable, like a bear or something.

He blew through the voice box, his ears alert to a recognizable sound, but what came out was unlike anything he'd heard before. His thoughts turned to death and rot. A screeching wail, the din felt surreal and otherworldly. Fingers clawed a chalkboard in a song of undulating rhythm. A song of shattered glass. When he stopped an odd sense of dread churned in his gut. He put the model on the counter, never taking his eyes away. Outside, the night swallowed the remainder of the day.

'That's no animal I've ever heard. Must be shaped wrong.'

A bang at the window made him jump. He whipped around to face the source of the shock, his heart thudding in his chest. He was surprised to see the glass hadn't shattered. Beyond the cabin's walls, a dark shape dropped to the porch.

He approached the glass with dragging feet, trying to swallow the nerves that jangled in his throat. The smell of the larynx turned sour in his nostrils. A bird. It had flown into the window. Snow covered the shape like powdered sugar. Ray cursed when it moved. The plump bird shuddered. Not much, but enough for Ray to know it was still alive.

'Damn, you hit it hard enough to break your neck. What were you running from, that you'd fly like a bat out of hell in a snowstorm?'

His gaze moved to the blizzard for an answer. Heavy whiteness dropped in wet clumps from the black heavens. He could see nothing, hear nothing, save silence (ear-killing silence) and the storm. For a moment he swore something moved out there. A dark figure, tall and lanky, drifted through the whiteout and vanished. Snow no doubt. Too tall to be a person anyway. A standing bear perhaps. He seemed to have them on his mind.

Ray went to the couch and shoved his bare feet into his nine-dollar Walmart sneakers. Coldness emanated from the front door, warning him to stay inside. He thought about his coffee in the kitchen, his unopened mail, and the novel he'd never write.

"'Why didn't you write, hon?" "Oh, a bird flew into the window, dear. Spent the whole time nursing the thing back to health." His hand reached for the door handle. "You know how I am about birds. What—you *don't* know? That my hermications aren't about writing at all, but *that*

I'll never tell you." "You lazy ass. You sneak away to nap and sit on the porch?" You'll *never* know that, dear.'

He'd have to come clean someday. Tell her he scrapped the book, or write something crappy, but first he'd milk these trips for a year or two longer if he could still afford it. Guilt is a bitch. He had too many friends like Chuck who used their education to their benefit. What had Ray done with his creative writing degree besides discover he hated writing? His dad would say he got wise and took on the family business like any good, hardworking American, only they weren't speaking now. He wouldn't hear what Pop had to say ever again at this point.

The world has enough books, Nick Jones told him over a steak dinner, *but there's never enough plumbers.*

Damn if Dad wasn't right. Jones Plumbing and Cooling paid for his house, kept the lights on at Number Twelve Pine Lane too, and would have put the girls through college if it hadn't been for that stupid fight. *Vote Red,* his dad yelled at him. Ray did the unthinkable, the *unforgivable sin* in the older Jones' book, after his pop shouted at him. He flipped him the bird. That simple act, that one middle finger (no different from the others really), ended things. And Ray had no idea what he'd do next. No idea what he'd tell Agatha.

The cold felt like a living, breathing beast when he opened the front door. Icy wings hugged him. A breath of stinging needles punctured his pores, making his skin congeal around his skull. Icy flakes pelted his skin and collected in his hair. His feet crunched in the frozen snow gathered on the porch. He pictured the ice scouring dried relish from the flannel, erasing the final clue to his gas station hot dog lunch. He could see the raven ahead and hurried to it, not wanting to be out in the elements any longer than necessary.

More snow accumulated on the bird's back and head, but he saw it move. Stunned and perhaps frozen, the bird would die before too long. Ray brushed the snow from it and quickly slid his fingers under its plump body. It made no move to defend itself.

'Bite away, big guy. Fingers are frozen. Won't feel a thing.' As he lifted it into his arms and made his way back to the door, he could see its head turn. Black eyes trained on his face. The raven's gaze didn't make his skin crawl, however. There was something else out there. Something far bigger, foul and clever, had him in its sights. Ray's gut told him as much. The dread squirmed like a gymnast in his belly. He slipped on the stoop, nearly falling over with his patient, before he stumbled inside and slammed the cabin door behind him. He hurried his patient to the kitchen and set it on the counter near the coffee maker and blue larynx. The wooden floorboards creaked under his soggy sneakers. He could feel the heat of the room wash over him. The flakes in his hair turned to water. The raven sat up on the counter but made no move to fly or run away. It kept his head lifted, watching him intently.

Unlike crows, ravens are more common in the sticks.

Not to mention bigger than crows. This guy could be a line-backer for an avian football league. A wet tuft of feathery hair hung over his bill. Another indication this creature wasn't a crow, but it also made him, or her, look a bit funny. Maybe it liked the moustache vibe. Ray grabbed an old dish towel from the cupboards and wrapped the fabric snugly around the bird. It watched him intently and made no sound.

After few sips of coffee, thankfully still warm, he reached into his jeans for his phone. He'd have to look this thing up. *If* he had a signal. Google had to know how to care for an injured bird. Text alerts caught his eye. He nearly clicked off, but the words cried out to be read. His sour stomach twisted into gruesome knots.

Ray, I can't get through to you on the phone. You need to answer!—Chuck.

Whatever you do, don't use that larynx. Don't blow into it. Don't even pick it up.—Chuck

Are you even getting my texts? Something happened when we used it. I can't explain. Don't use that larynx.—Chuck

Footsteps crunched on the snow outside. Something was on the porch. The phone slipped from his fingers and clattered to the floor. Ray gave it no thought. Instead he took a step toward the window. The footsteps continued but he could see nothing. It sounded close. Right outside the door. Ray's eyes moved to the entry. Had he locked the door?

He ran to it. The lock was upright. Sideways locked,

upright unlocked.

It creaked open just as he got there.

A blue-white shape reached inside. Long arms, longer than any human's, clawed at him. Ray's mind went numb. Behind him, the raven made an unnatural mewling sound. Ray himself made a similar sound when the tendrils at the end of the arm found purchase on his collar. He couldn't focus. Couldn't see more than a blue-white shape, like the arm of a squid slithering in the air, but what that arm connected to he couldn't make out. Its touch was as cold as ice. He felt glaciers spread in his body, from his neck down. A fog blanketed his mind.

'Out. Get out . . . ' he heard himself speak. His voice sounded different, more like a choked frog than his normal deep utterances. This wasn't something that would understand his words. He knew that. Even groggy with sub-zero terror, he knew it wouldn't stop. His eyes focused for the briefest moment, long enough to see the rest of the creature. Icy blue, as if sculpted from snow; it stood at least eight feet tall. It would have to stoop low to enter. He could feel the tendril-hand constrict over his throat. The shape was like that of a man. Tall and lanky, like a scarecrow with long octopus arms. Only he saw no discernible face. No mouth, no eyes. No nose, no ears . . . He flailed his arms, slapping limply, and to no avail.

How could it be standing here? What the hell was it?

Visions of warmth seeped into his mind. The tundra turned to summer. A hot blackness replaced the horror before him. He welcomed it. Wanted it in fact. When the icy octopus arm began to cut into his neck, Ray Jones barely noticed. Blood seeped in a congealed mass, like pudding, from the slit.

The raven landed on the blue-white flesh. Its claws dug in and its beak tore at the material that made up the abomination's form. Spaghetti strands of fleshy ice came from the long arm and blue tendons convulsed and retracted. The coil around Ray's throat fell away. The horror withdrew into the darkness outside.

Ray stumbled backward like a drunk who'd just walked into a wall. The fog receded from his mind and he struggled to remain standing.

The raven fluttered and screeched at the thing. Black feathers filled Ray's vision. He managed to grab the bird and pull it away. He kicked the door shut. Somehow his hand flicked the lock. Sideways. Safe. But for how long?

Stumbling back into the warmth of the cabin, Ray turned to the kitchen. The raven flew from his arms to the kitchen counter. It flew in a black arc, landed gracefully, and made a croaking sound. Ray followed, though he didn't know why, but knew he needed to clean the cut at his neck. Find a first aid kit. The raven bounced excitedly on the towel. Ray's gaze wandered to the oesophagus. His mind cleared.

He grabbed his cell phone and dialled 9-1-1. Nothing. He checked the reception. Not a single damn bar. The front door shook on its hinges. It wanted in. The sound of its icy hammering echoed through the cabin.

Ray turned to face the window and saw only whiteness. The raven excitedly fluttered into the air and landed on his right shoulder. Ray's pulse beat heavily in his chest. He grabbed the towel and dabbed at his neck. The raven gargled in his ear. Only a bit of blood came off. He picked up the 3-D model. Had the bird come to him for comfort, recognizing safety in numbers?

At that moment, with his paperback nearby, Ray came up with a name for the bird.

'Herbert, what the hell is that thing?' he asked. It nuzzled the greying hair at the back of his head. He saw the tall shape at the kitchen window. It drifted like a blowing sheet into the weak kitchen light cast onto the porch.

The glass shattered in an explosion of cold wind and ice. Shards shot past him and the bird.

Ray ran from the room as the creature lowered its upper torso and entered. Long arms ending in blue-white octopus fingers grabbed the window's edge. Ray made it as far as the fireplace when his legs gave out. The raven clung to his ratty flannel as he crumpled in front of the roaring flames. Both turned to face the creature climbing into the kitchen.

The horror approached on two spindly legs, faceless head lowered. Now, Ray saw it clearly. It wasn't entirely faceless after all. A gash across the jaw gaped open; cold gusts of air formed steamy clouds with each breath. Its body seemed to be made of ice—sinewy, fleshy ice. Blue veins wove around the muscles and extremities. A long neck carried a pea shaped head. How could it see with no eyes, hear with no ears?

As it clambered over the kitchen table, a whirl of snow flurries in the kitchen behind it, its small head turned to face its prey. It followed him on gliding legs. A kitchen chair fell over behind it.

Ray struggled to get to his feet, but found he no longer had the strength. The raven stayed with him, its claws digging into his shoulder. He dropped his cell phone and the oesophagus. Both clattered to the ground. He watched the creature approach, tensing for the icy touch. The fireplace sent baking warmth into his back. The heat washed over his cheeks. Any longer and he'd have a roasted bird on his shoulder.

The giant came to a stop. Where it had moved forward, gliding on slithery feet, now it moved no further. The grim mouth froze. Its grossly long arms hung limp. And a small puddle of water expanded across the floor near its claw-like feet.

The raven fluffed on Ray's shoulder. Cold drops of melting snow spattered his cheeks.

'The fireplace,' Ray surmised. 'The heat. Doesn't like it.' The bird gurgled quietly in his ear.

Tense, the blaze scorching the back of his neck, Ray waited for those octopus fingers to attack. The creature made no attempt to hurt him. The heat of the fire formed

223

a protective aura. Ray wondered how long it would hold. For now the fire appeared to be a ward, but when the flames died down?

He waited five minutes, ten minutes, half an hour, and finally glanced away from the creature. It had not moved. Herbert remained a silent sentinel on his shoulder.

The small logs were within easy reach and, thank God, situated on a black wrought iron base within the aura of heat. The raven stirred slightly when Ray reached to the base, grabbing a plump log. It offered no indication it was a terrible malevolent being. The blue giant might very well have been a cursed statue carved of ice. The reflection of orange and red flames danced on its featureless face. He tossed the log atop the fire, hearing the flames spit and crackle.

His proximity to the fire felt unbearable at times. Ray stayed rooted. As did the raven. It, too, preferred the uncomfortable heat over an agonizing, icy death.

Another twenty minutes went by. The creature still had not moved. Snow began to form white, clumpy drifts on the kitchen table and floor near the shattered kitchen window. Ray found his fingers tracing the length of the model by his feet. The eeriness of the sound it emitted had to have drawn the giant. Had it also drawn the raven?

He reached behind and tossed another log onto the fire. One wanted to kill him. He wondered how long he and his protector would last. When no more logs remained to heat the fireplace, when the living room turned as cold as the empty stretch of snow-covered Pine Lane outside, he'd find the squid fingers once more wrapped around his throat.

Ray remembered the dreadful feeling when he used the larynx earlier. He held the model against his chest. The blue plastic felt warm to the touch. Dare he risk it again? Perhaps in his tired, terrified mind, the logic seemed right. Ray pulled the piece to his sweating face and the bird gurgled once again. If it knew the model were to blame it gave no sign of it, nor did it try to stop him.

'Have to think good thoughts,' Ray whispered. 'Order it to go away.'

His voice turned chilly cold as he spoke through the model. Ribbons of cold revulsion slithered from his shoulders to his waist. Only he didn't stop. He told the creature to leave. Leave and never return. He pleaded with it. He forced his mind to dwell on smiles and gratitude. Harder to conjure than fear and death. Sweat dripped from his brow into his eye, causing him to blink. As he did, the creature undulated as if dancing to music only it could hear. A black shape soared into the room, followed by another and another. Three ravens, as big as Ray's companion, swooped into the kitchen, flying gracefully through the kitchen into the living room. Their arrival excited Herbert.

His new friend sprang to the wooden floor, bouncing up and down, and snapped its black beak as if sending a message in Morse Code. The creature lashed out, arms raised and body lunging forward, trying to snare the birds.

Each managed to evade its grasp, one snagging a tendril of flesh from the giant's shoulder, before landing at Ray's feet. The creature lunged at them, but stopped short of the fire's protective glow. As Ray lowered the larynx from his lips, the creature receded to its original position. The ravens chattered vigorously with each other.

Ray's confusion at the ravens' appearance turned to cold fear when a snowy shape ducked low to enter through the kitchen. Another tall horror, identical to the first, had been summoned.

He heard glass shatter on the far side of the living room. Shards skittered to a stop at the raven's claws. A third creature. A fourth then emerged from the back end of the living room, having smashed through the back door. Ray's mind turned to putty at the realization of his misdeeds. He struggled to comprehend the existence of such beings, yet found his mind wincing in pain when he tried. Four ravens, four giants. Ray's mind settled on his impending death instead.

He stood, refusing to make himself an easy target, and the ravens gathered at his feet. Why he thought standing would be a better way to die, he didn't know, but the position felt more defiant. *Take it like a man,* his father would say. The birds were hopping in place, staring at the creatures and gurgling; almost taunting the giants. They weren't interested in the birds, or Ray for that matter.

The icy monstrosities had no sooner entered the room

together when they began to fight. They lunged, making no sound, and wrapped their tendrils around one another. Arms, hands, neck, made no difference.

Two slammed against the wall, cracking the wood, and knocked an old white clock off the wall. Yellow with age, the long-dead clock broke into jagged fragments when it landed.

The giants slapped and swiped at one another. A tendril, then a second and third, lopped off and flew toward the fireplace. The appendages slid into the aura of fire. Two of the ravens grabbed them and, with a quick flick of the beak, tossed them out of the circle of warmth. The appendages started to melt as soon as they entered the heat zone, as if the creatures were indeed made of liquid. The giants made no sound other than the ruckus caused by their battle. When two were killed, the survivors fell snarling into combat with each other. Their vicious battle lasted for more than ten minutes. Number Twelve Pine Lane looked as if a bomb had detonated in the centre of the place. The creatures threw each other against walls and broke furniture, always silent, their gash mouths twisted into snarls of hate. They fell in a storm of razor-sharp tentacles atop the old loveseat. The seat snapped at the centre like the dried branch of a long-dead tree. Finally, one of the giants rolled away from the melee. The other made no move at all and Ray saw why. Most of its head had been severed from its neck. Only a sliver of snow-white flesh connected the two.

The last surviving giant, perhaps the original creature, moved slowly near the aura of the fireplace. It struggled to get up. While its legs remained, the white terror had only a single arm. Lacerations covered its frozen body.

The ravens flew into action. With a loud croaking noise, they left the protective ring of the fire and dove headlong into battle with the creature. The birds made quick work of what remained. Their powerful beaks tore the icy flesh to ribbons, claws separated blue-white tendons from its body. The giant had but one arm to defend itself, with only a few tendrils left to slice. The birds easily took the horror down. The last of the giants soon thumped against the floor, face planted into the cold puddle of a melted arm. A few black feathers drifted to the floor around it.

Ray refused to believe the threat was over. He stood rooted to the spot for half an hour. He tossed new logs onto the pile to increase the heat, terrified to leave, despite his scorched skin. The ravens made their unusual "gronk gronk" noises and hopped around the once cosy living room.

His bladder made him take the first step. Before leaving the ring of warmth he held one end of a hand-sized log to the fire. Once the end blazed a halo of warmth around him, he made his way through the cabin, wincing with every curtain pulled back and every closet door opened. He was alone. He visited the bathroom upstairs, holding the torch over his head as he urinated, before returning to the bodies on the first floor. The ravens were lined up in a row on the mantel.

Ray held the torch to the lifeless giants to ensure they were truly dead. Their flesh melted under the torch's heat as quickly as Baum's Wicked Witch. He moved from body to body until nothing remained of the violent creatures but water. The ravens watched him in silence. The four seemed tired and content to enjoy their own toasty hermication.

Ray retrieved his cell phone from the floor in front of the fireplace, noting he still had no service, and only fifteen percent of life left, then scooped up the 3-D larynx. He considered chucking it into the fire. He could watch it burn, the blue plastic sending curling black smoke into the chimney, and find contentment that it would never again call forth the foul beasts.

A sly grin crept across his stubbled face. His fingers tightened around the oesophagus. Would it work in Phoenix?

Next time his father said, 'I'm cutting you from the will. I'll not let a damn liberal inherit my money. No commie gonna run my business. Blah-blah-blah,' Ray would have an answer.

'Hold on a second, Pop. Try blowing in this here bad boy. You'll love it. But you have to wait until I've gone.' He'd then have the cash to repair Number Twelve Pine Lane. He might even have an idea or two for that Great American Novel, which he was certain Herbert would help him write.

COME BACK

A LIMERICK
TO ACCOMPANY
'THE BURNING BOY'
BY DENVER GRENELL

When the wind blows cold and the snowflakes fall
And dead leaves float from trees so tall
When the days grow short and the nights are black
The Burning Boy comes back, comes back

At first so faint between the trees
A flickering candle light it seems
Through woodlands thick and night so black,
The Burning Boy comes back, comes back

It is he, the one who burns
With red wrath the demon churns
His flames dance along the beaten track
The Burning Boy is back, is back

Draw your curtains and bolt your doors
Who does he come for? Whose name is called?
And should he stop before your shack

Your time is short alas, alack
Through woodlands thick and night so black
The Burning Boy comes back, comes back
Your time is short alas alack
The Burning Boy is back, is back

YULETIDETIME

A POEM
TO ACCOMPANY
'THE WILD HUNT'

BY ROXIE VOORHEES

Snow came down at Yuletide,
Snow all dainty, Snow flurry;
Snow innate at Yuletide
Mistletoe gave no worry.

The Wild Hunt flies on by
Snow cold as Hel, Snow flurry;
The Wild Hunt's stormy sky
Valkyries gave no worry.

All Lost Souls to gather,
Stay inside tonight surely;
Hail Odin! Hail All-father!
Warm Wassail gave no worry.

LITTLE BILLY'S NAUGHTY CHRISTMAS

A STORY
BY SPENCER HAMILTON

Little Billy McCreedy had a propensity for sleepwalking, and it was this affliction that brought him out of bed in the witching hour of Christmas Eve.

Billy's family had grown used to his wandering around in the dead of night, a zombified, slack expression on his face, pale in the sparse moonlight; they had grown used to sleeping through his little bumps in the night as he staggered through the hallways of their Victorian home, shambling around in his pyjamas until he had exorcised whatever restless demons which had plucked him from bed.

That is why, on the Christmas Eve of Billy's eighth year, he woke to find himself alone in the foyer. Moonlight spread a kaleidoscope of colours on the gleaming cherrywood before his socked feet as it shone through the stained-glass pane above the double-entrance doors. It all looked rather festive to Billy, infusing his foggy, sleep-addled brain with Christmas spirit. He was warm from head to toe, nice and cosy in his holly-chequered PJs. All was quiet and serene.

So what had wakened him from his sleepwalking?

Tap-tap.

Something was knocking. Not on the front doors, but on the narrow pane of glass that ran along their length to the side.

Tap . . . tap-tap-tap.

Billy peered closer. Was that . . ?

'Santa!'

Billy clasped a hand over his mouth and giggled. But no one stirred upstairs. His family had truly grown used to his midnight excursions.

Tap-tap.

And it *was* Santa. Right there, just a few feet away and on the other side of the glass. Just like he'd imagined: red velvet coat cinched over a great belly, a great big beard, and rosy cheeks.

But what was Santa doing at the front door?

Quietly, Billy stepped forward and turned the bolt. He clasped the big, filigreed handle with both hands and swung the door open. It came inward without a sound, and a gust of icy air ruffled his pyjamas and made him shiver.

He stared into the dark. Their front porch light should have clicked on at the slightest movement, but everything remained draped in shadow.

'Santa . . ?' Billy whispered, squinting his eyes against the breeze.

There was no answer, but through the silence came the sound of heavy, ragged breathing. Billy blinked a few times, willing his eyes to see in the dark, and slowly, shapes coalesced from the shadows. A big, dark red mass swam towards him from out of the night, and the velvet he'd seen through the window was clearer now: matted and dirty, one frayed corner caked in something that smelled suspiciously of shit. Slung across the red expanse was a black belt that reminded Billy of the belt his daddy had used on him that one time, but he didn't like thinking about that.

The ragged breaths hitched, and from the grinning face above the red velvet coat spilled out a cloud of condensation, dispersing as it hit the warm air directly over the threshold.

'Ho . . . ho . . . ho,' the grinning face said.

Another shiver passed down Billy's spine.

'Santa, is that really you?'

The man's grin widened, showing yellowed and blackened teeth and one glinting spot of gold. 'It ain't the Easter bunny, kiddo.'

Billy giggled again, though now his mirth was spiked with a hint of unease. Santa looked . . . off. And there was that nagging question of why he was at the front door.

'But why are you here, Santa?'

The man bent with his hands on his knees, and now Billy could see his fingernails were caked with something dark and flaky, and Santa's breath made his eyes sting.

'You're a smart lad,' breathed Santa. 'You know what day it is? Or ...' He made a show of looking over his shoulder at the empty, quiet neighbourhood then grinned sheepishly. 'Night.'

Billy knew the answer to *that*. 'It's Christmas Eve, of course!'

Santa winked at him. 'Right you are, lad.'

'But I mean, why are you *here*? At the front door? You're supposed to go down the *chimney*, silly.'

Santa seemed, for a moment, caught off guard, and it was during this pause that Billy finally noticed just how incredibly filthy Santa's beard was. It was nothing like those white nylon things shopping-mall Santas wore—because it was *real*, he told himself, and those other Santas were just volunteering while the real Santa busied himself with the naughty-or-nice list. Still, this beard was knotted and tangled and unwashed, shot through with scraggly greys and blacks. There seemed to be bits of food trapped in it.

'Would you believe it,' Santa said, 'but the dang thing is clogged.'

Billy blinked in surprise, forgetting the beard. 'Clogged?'

Santa took a step closer, still bent over. 'Truth is, kiddo, your dad sealed it off with quick-dry cement. He decided you were being too naughty to get a visit from Santa.'

A brief memory flashed in Billy's mind: the sting that came with the cracking sound of Daddy's belt.

Billy whispered, his voice squeaking: 'He did?'

Another flash: his daddy's rough voice, saying over and over, *Naughty, Billy, naughty naughty naughty—*

'Hey, cheer up, kiddo,' Santa said, and Billy got his first whiff of the man's breath: rancid, like the dead dog the other boys had shown him near the fence behind the playground (he'd refused to poke it with a stick like the others, not saying but deeply fearing that this would put him on Santa's naughty list).

– naughty, Billy, naughty naughty—

'Cheer up, ya wanna know why?' Santa's gold tooth winked in the darkness of that rancid mouth, winked almost conspiratorially. 'Because your daddy was wrong. You ain't naughty.'

Relief rushed through Billy, banishing the chill that had begun to creep in from the open doorway. 'I'm not?'

'Of course not! Why do you think you happened to be the one to let me inside?'

Billy blinked, confused.

'*Magic*, kiddo,' Santa breathed.

Billy gaped at Santa. Of *course*. It wasn't the *tap-tapping* on the glass that had woken him. It was Santa's magic. Probably it was Santa's magic that made him sleepwalk down here in the first place. Because Daddy was *wrong*; Billy wasn't naughty . . . Billy was nice!

He peered down at Santa's feet, just noticing the burlap sack cinched closed with a frayed, scratchy rope and leaning against Santa's scuffed and torn boot. It looked suspiciously too small to hold the PlayStation or electric guitar he'd asked for, but appearances could be deceiving when *magic* was involved.

'You need help with those presents, Santa?'

The man laughed, a sickly, coughing spurt that plumed condensation past the threshold like dragon's breath.

'Santa's got that covered, kiddo. But whaddaya say we get this party started and you let me in?'

There was a moment where something about all of this sounded a warning klaxon in Billy's brain. Perhaps it was the stuff caked in Santa's fingernails, which looked more and more like blood as his eyes adjusted to the dark. And speaking of the dark, what happened to the front porch lights? Maybe Santa's magic cloaked him from such things, but they should have blinked on as soon as the front door opened.

But then the moment was gone and Billy stepped back to let Santa Claus inside.

'Rise and shine, motherfucker. Up and at 'em, whaddaya say?'

Reginald and Lucille McCreedy woke to a nightmare.

The first thing they saw was deceptively picturesque: their beautiful little boy, Billy, beaming and aglow in his flannel pyjamas, with a silver fir draped in tinsel rising above him in a warm wash of icicle lights.

But then the nightmare lurched into their vision, and

Lucy screamed. A seething, pockmarked face covered in a film of grime and a mat of rank beard hair. It was grinning at them, a maniac's glee shining from the bulging eyes. And sitting atop it was . . .

A Santa Claus hat?

'Ho . . . ho . . . ho . . . *Merrrrrrrry* Christmassss.'

Lucy, unable to look the nightmare directly in the eye, turned to her boy.

'Billy . . . sweety . . . what's going on?'

Billy stayed where he was, smiling serenely at her, and said words that sent a shiver down Lucille McCreedy's spine:

'Daddy's been naughty.'

'Daddy's been . . ?' Lucy switched to her stern voice. 'Billy, come untie me at once!'

For she was, absurdly, tied to a chair. One of the uncomfortable polished straight-back ones from the dining room, dragged here in the sitting room where it didn't belong. She was in her nightgown, it was only God knew how early in the morning, or perhaps still the middle of the night. For wasn't it the darkest part of the night that nightmares came out to play?

'I can't, Mommy,' Billy said, still smiling. 'Santa says.'

Santa says . . .

Like some sick version of Simon Says, her boy was now taking orders not from his mother but from this madman, this filthy vagrant calling himself Saint Nicholas.

'It'll all come clear soon enough, love,' the vagrant

breathed, bending closer to brush her cheek with one mangy paw. She coughed from the fumes on his breath. 'Shh, shh, that's it, shhhh . . .'

He turned and thudded one scuffed boot into her husband's side. She watched helplessly as thick curds of black mud flecked from the boot and flurried down across the carpet. Her beautiful, fluffy carpet, hand-chosen and textured—real wool, though now she wished she'd gone with the more durable nylon, or even polyester. Tracked through that field of freshly-fallen-snow carpet were large craters of mud. The madman's muddy boot prints, pressed with perfect preservation like a charcoal rubbing of a headstone. Stains that would surely never come out.

Reginald coughed himself awake, groaning with pain. 'What in the bloody—'

'Merry Christmas, Daddy!' Billy exclaimed.

'Bill, what the devil—'

'Aye, Daddy-O, Merry fuckin' Christmas, eh?' the madman seethed.

'I demand you,' Reginald barked, though the bite had already begun to drain from his voice, 'whatever this nonsense is—'

'This *nonsense*,' said the madman. 'You hear what your daddy calls me, Billy? 'Nonsense' indeed. Ask him if the chimney's nonsense, go on.'

Billy, still grinning that grin that Lucille had begun to associate with some other creature that *looked* like her boy but surely wasn't, stepped closer to Reginald in his socked feet and said, 'I know about the chimney, Daddy. Santa told me.'

'The chimney . . ? Bill, what the hell is this?'

The smile never faltered on the boy's chubby little face. 'You don't have to pretend anymore, Daddy. Santa knows. 'He sees you when you're sleeping', right?' Little Billy giggled.

'Right-O indeed, m'boy,' the madman said.

'You do not speak to my son,' Reginald barked, adopting his stern voice Lucille overheard during his phone calls from within his office. 'I'll have you know you've dug yourself into deep shit from which the police will not allow you to—'

But as her husband continued with his stern, lecturing voice, Lucille watched in horror as the man masquerading as Santa turned to her son—her little boy, Little Billy—and nodded and winked, as if the two were in on a little secret, and Billy slapped his own father.

'William Jacob McCreedy!' Lucille shrieked.

Billy looked at her, and for the first time she noticed a mean glint to that smile. 'He said a naughty word, Mommy.'

'That he did, kiddo, that he did,' the madman said.

'YOU DO NOT SPEAK TO MY SON!' Reginald roared.

The madman barked with laughter. 'Talks a big game for someone caught in his undies, eh, Bill?'

Billy giggled.

What followed was an obscenely absurd moment, one

Lucille would likely never forget. This madman and her own sweet little boy, doubled over with mocking, mirthful laughter, pointing at her husband's night clothes: a white undershirt (that admittedly wasn't so white at the pits) and tighty-whities (that, also admittedly, weren't so white near certain extremities). The indignation of it all was too much to bear; what if they turned next to Lucille's nightgown and guffawed their mockery at *her*? She would *die*.

Reginald coughed awkwardly, as if clearing his throat to pardon some indiscretion, and the stern tone in his voice honed itself to a point: 'Sir, how dare you? Do you know who I am?'

Still bent over from laughing, the man dressed in a Santa suit plucked a horrid burlap sack from Lucille's ruined carpet and in the same motion swung it into Reginald's face. Her husband's scream was muffled by metallic clinks from within the bag.

Billy, also, cried out in alarm, and Lucille felt a rush of relief: finally, her boy had remembered his polite upbringing and would help untie them and end this charade.

But she was hopelessly wrong. For the words that came out of Billy's mouth were not full of concern for the wellbeing of his father, but for the contents of the bag.

'My presents!'

'It's all right, kiddo,' the Santa said. 'Won't do them no harm. Magic, remember?'

The smile reasserted itself on her boy's face, and he whispered, 'Magic.'

Reginald was no longer screaming—he was no longer doing *anything*, in fact; just sitting there, his face etched in disbelief, the only movement a fat drop of blood as it trickled down from the hard ridge of his eyebrow and into the stress lines around his mouth, which was slightly open.

Santa—Lucille hated thinking of this madman as such, but it was all just so *absurd*—tossed the burlap sack back down and stepped back towards Reginald.

'Reginald ... William ... McCreedy,' Santa said, slow and deliberate. 'Attorney-at-law, soon going partner at the firm Johnson, Johnson & Sons. Yes, I bloody well know who you are.'

Reginald, who had twitched at every part of his own name, blinked. More blood fell, spilling into his mouth, but he didn't seem to notice. 'How .. ?'

'Because he's *Santa*, Daddy!' Billy exclaimed, and then he burst into song: *'He sees you when you're sleeping! He knows when you're awake!'*

'Billy, dear,' Lucille broke in, 'please, Mommy has a headache—'

But Little Billy only raised his voice further. *'He knows when you've been bad or good, so be good for goodness' sake!'*

Santa put a hand on Billy's shoulder, which did the trick to silence him, and returned his grin to Reginald. 'You better watch out, Reggie, old man, hey?'

'Sir, please,' Lucille spoke up. She was loathe to speak in her husband's place, but surely this had gone on long enough. 'Whatever your … grievances, surely we can come to some understanding. Surely there's no need for such violence. On Christmas morning, no less!' She forced out an awkward little titter, as if laughing at such vulgarity would sweep it under the proverbial rug.

'Oh,' answered Santa, 'I think there's plenty need. Wouldn't you say, kiddo?'

Her son grinned back.

'How do you know me?' Reginald asked. His voice was low, defeated. 'What has my family ever done to you, sir?'

'Ah, 'sir' now, is it?' Santa laughed as he lowered himself into the wingback chair by the hearth. She'd never get those stains out. 'Well, that's a step in the right direction, wouldn't ya say, Bill?'

Her son grinned back.

'Why don't you tell them, kiddo?' Santa went on, really and truly settling into the leather of the armchair. Lucille flinched at every flake of mud as it dusted her furniture. 'Tell your folks just what brought Jolly Ol' Saint Nick to the McCreedy residence via the front door?'

Little Billy stood in his holly-berry PJs in front of the fireplace, which at that moment was unlit, just a cold, black hole wreathed in shadows, and Lucille realised just how cold she was. Goosebumps plucked her flesh beneath the light cloth of her nightgown, exacerbated by that queer smile on her little boy's face. She shivered.

Billy cleared his throat and, absurdity in a night filled with the absurd, began to recite a poem.

''Twas the night before Christmas,' he began, his voice high and clear, *'when all through the house, not a creature was stirring, not even a mouse.'* He paused, a gleeful gleam in his eye. 'Or that's how it was *supposed* to go. But one creature *did* stir . . . me!' Billy beamed at his parents. 'The magic that Santa Claus uses to get presents to all the nice little boys and girls sent me on one of my sleepwalking episodes and then woke me at the front door.'

'Bill, son, stop,' Reginald muttered, his voice still soft, still defeated. And in that moment, Lucille found herself loathing the sound of such a weak voice.

'Santa's magic knew he would need a little helper,' Billy went on, ignoring his father's pleas. 'And so it sent *me*, and I let Santa in so he could give Sally and me our Christmas presents!'

At the mention of her daughter's name, Lucille felt a low moan rise up from her gut. Sally . . . her sweet little Sally . . . *Dear God,* she prayed, *please let my Sally not be a part of this.*

'That's not Santa, Bill,' Reginald said. 'Can't you see? Not Santa.'

But Billy was unfazed. 'Santa told me you'd say that, Daddy. Santa told me you'd say *anything* to keep from admitting the truth.'

'What truth, Billy?' Lucille said, if only to stop that moan before it turned into a scream. 'Tell Mommy the truth, baby, what truth is it?'

The Christmas lights hugging the tree shone pinprick reflections in her boy's eyes as he said, 'Daddy's been naughty.'

Silence fell as they took that in.

'Bill, lad,' Reginald said, 'that's just for boys and girls. The whole 'naughty or nice' thing, it's just a child's song. To keep you and your baby sister on your best behaviour.'

A flash of anger flitted across Billy's face. 'But you *said*. It was just an accident but you *said*.'

Tears sprang to her boy's eyes. Lucille had never seen such sudden emotion from Billy. Her Sally, certainly, but Billy had always behaved in less erratic, more muted ways. And he'd certainly never said anything to her about an "accident".

'What is it, Billy?' she asked. 'What accident?'

Reginald's stern voice came back: 'Bill—'

'*He sees you when you're sleeping!*' Billy shouted at his father.

'It's just a silly song, Bill.'

'I only saw on accident,' Billy went on, tears now streaming down his chubby face, 'but you said—you said *I* was naughty. Which meant ... which meant ... I'd get *coal*—'

Reginald struggled in his chair. 'SANTA CLAUS ISN'T BLOODY REAL!'

Billy turned away from his parents, blubbering, and huddled closer to the man who had convinced their child

250

he was Santa Claus. The man didn't pat him on the shoulder, didn't comfort him in any way. He put both grimy hands on either side of the boy's face, looked him dead in the eye, and said:

'You've got the magic, kiddo.'

The boy turned back to them, a new resolve on his face. 'I saw Daddy sleeping with a pretty lady who wasn't Mommy and he took the belt to me.'

Silence descended once more.

Sleeping with a pretty lady . . ? Lucille blinked, horrified. The boy was confused. He couldn't mean—

'Just a dream, Bill,' Reginald said, though that stern tone had drained away. 'You were sleepwalking again—'

'*No!*' Billy yelled. 'I *saw* you and you *beat* me! And you called me naughty, but *you're* naughty, Daddy, *you* are!'

The Santa had risen from the armchair and was kneeling behind their son now, one arm slung comfortingly around his shoulders. 'All right, kiddo, whaddaya say that's enough? I've gotta get to all the other boys and girls tonight, so why don't we speed this up, eh?'

Billy smeared one hand across his tear-stained face and nodded.

'I think it's time to open that sack of presents, huh?' Santa said. 'Why don't you go lay everything out across the carpet while I have some last words with the ol' Mommy and Daddy?'

The smile had returned to Little Billy's face. In the most horrifying moment of the whole absurd nightmare,

Lucille watched her own child turn and embrace this disgusting madman with all the love he possessed. He then proceeded to turn to the Christmas tree, where he collected the burlap sack from the carpet, sat Indian-style next to the prettily wrapped gifts already beneath the tree, and stuck his hand inside the sack.

Her view of her boy disappeared as this Santa Claus from Hell stepped closer. She tried to hold her breath, but his reek withered her nose hairs.

'Listen closely, you motherfucker,' he breathed, and Lucille was ashamed at the wash of relief she felt at seeing he was speaking to Reginald, not her. 'And if you interrupt me to say a single word I'll take this nine-millimetre Luger from my belt and silence you for good. We clear?'

Reginald nodded, silent. The blood dripping down his face splashed onto the arm of the chair he was tied to.

'Atta boy,' Santa said. 'Your boy here is smart. I *am* Santa Claus, and I *do* have magic, though this Kringle ain't the one from the stories. This one is from your worst nightmares.'

Lucille whimpered, that moan finally clawing its fingers up her throat.

'Your lad caught you, Reg. You're good and caught, and there's no denying it.'

Reginald did not so much as make a sound.

Santa turned to Lucille. 'Your hubby here got himself good and truly fucked, he did, and yes, I'm talking about the kind of 'fucked' where he gets hisself a prostitute and ass-fucks her in his own bed. *Your* bed. But he's too daft to check his family's schedule and realise his kiddies are in the playroom, and when one o' them walks in on the, shall we say, *transaction*, what does he do?'

In the silence that followed, Lucille's mind was blank. She refused, absolutely refused to believe that her Reginald would bring such filth into their home, and how *dare* this stranger—

'Ah, smart, Reg,' Santa said. 'I ask you a question but you stay good and quiet lest I blow yer brains out yer arse. Rhetorical, it was. What ol' Reggie here does is take a big ol' belt to his own child, beat him till he's completely cried out and can't say a word, the whole while telling li'l Bill that he's *naughty*, that he will never say a word of this to anyone.'

The man grinned at them both.

'But don't worry. Santy Claus knows all.'

Billy's voice from behind: 'It's ready, Santa!'

Santa turned to him, said, 'All right, atta boy, kiddo, just gimme one more mo',' then turned back to Reginald. 'So Reggie here beats 'is own child for catching you with your willy wet. But the old man ain't done there, is he? He's gotta bury his own shame by lashing out at everyone else, ain't that right?'

Lucille whimpered again. 'What in heavens is this man talking about, Reginald?'

'Ah-ah-ahhh,' Santa said, playfully slapping Reginald in the face. 'Best not to answer her. I didn't give her the same rule of silence, though I can't say this ends well for her, either.'

Before Lucille's frozen mind could attempt to parse the meaning of these words, Santa's next words shot a spike of pure shock through her spinal cord.

'Your husband sent his prostitute packing without paying his bill, threatened her with lawsuits from his firm, used the ol' Johnson, Johnson & Son name to throw around his weight, then, as if that weren't enough, had the pretty lady murdered.'

Reginald's face was unreadable, yet Lucille couldn't stand to look at it.

It can't be true.

But she knew it was. Lucille McCreedy, née Jones, had lived in fear of her husband long enough to understand what he was capable of.

'But don't you worry your little heads,' Santa said, straightening up and grinning down at both Reginald and Lucille in turn. 'Santa's here to make sure your kiddos have a Christmas they'll never forget.'

He turned from them and joined Billy, and now Lucille could see what her son had dragged from within the burlap sack: laid out in meticulous order across the fluffy carpet were tools. Sharp, metal tools, gleaming in places and rusted in others, of all shapes and sizes but most of which ended in serrated edges and sharp points.

'All right, m'boy,' Santa said. 'My little Santa's helper. Whaddaya say we get the presents ready for you and Sal'?'

When Billy straightened up, a rusty serrated saw clutched in his little hands, Lucille saw that strange grin on his face again, and she fainted.

Sally woke with the first rays of sunlight streaming through her curtains, and her first thought was:

It's Christmas morning!

Closely followed by her second thought, upon seeing the sunlight:

Billy let me sleep in!

Ugh. How could he? He *knew* this was her favourite day of the year. She put up with his constant bumping around at night, learned to sleep through all the noise of his sleepwalking; the least he could do was wake her up before dawn on Christmas like she'd asked.

'Billy?' she whispered. It was tradition for them to creep downstairs past their parents' bedroom door and rifle through their stocking goodies quietly together; perhaps it still wasn't too late for that. 'Billy, you up?'

Nothing. His bed, on the other side of the room, stood empty. His slippers sat discarded on the floor, which meant he hadn't come back from his latest sleepwalking episode.

She sighed, stuffed her feet into her own slippers—fluffy and pink and made to look like little wedges of cake—and shuffled quietly into the hall.

The house was unnaturally quiet. Usually by the time

sunlight kissed the windows, Mommy and Daddy came down the stairs and she and Billy woke them up fully with a loud cry of *'Merry Christmas!'* Why was this year different?

She paused halfway down the staircase and stifled a giggle. Maybe Billy had sleepwalked smack-dab into the middle of Mommy and Daddy setting out all of their presents. She was only six, but Sally learned last week from Ellie at school that Santa Claus was just a fairy-tale. Mommy had made Sally keep it a secret when she'd brought it up, said Billy still believed. So how *funny* it must have been for him to bump into them filling his stocking and eating the cookies and milk he'd set out for some fat guy in a suit. She giggled again, clamping both hands over her mouth.

Maybe that was why none of the others were up yet. They were all tuckered out from breaking the news to Bill about Santa Claus, and they were sleeping it off in Mommy and Daddy's room. Bill was a little old to sleep in the same bed as Mommy and Daddy, but then, Sally reasoned, he was a little old to still believe in Santa Claus, too . . .

'*Merry Christmas, Sally!*'

As she turned the corner into the sitting room, she found Billy in his PJs and on the carpet, all alone. The fire was roaring and there was a weird smell, and if Bill was being so loud already then where were Mommy and Daddy?

'Bill . . .'

He burst up from the carpet and grabbed her in a big

bear hug, and by the end of it she was squealing and squirming for him to put her down, that she was *ticklish*, stop it, Big Bill!

When he finally did put her down and let her go, her giggles diminished to confusion as she noticed . . . Billy was *sticky*. His fingers came away from her PJs reluctantly, and his own pyjamas were mucked up and peeled away from hers as an afterthought. Like he'd gotten into the kitchen and licked the raspberry pie pan clean.

And sure enough, as she got a closer look at her brother's face, she saw the raspberry smeared around his mouth, big wet gobs of it stuck to his lips and cheeks and dribbling from his chin. Raspberry, except . . . *off*.

'Bill . . . what's that stuff on your face and your fingers? Breakfast?'

A stab of jealousy: *Did he* eat *without me, too?*

Bill lifted his pyjama shirt to wipe his face and mouth. The soft, pale white of his belly struck Sally as stark in comparison with the rest of the scene, though she wasn't sure why.

Bill didn't answer her question. After wiping his face, he took her hand in his—still sticky, she noticed, and she had the urge to snatch her hand away—and he marched her over to the fireplace, saying, enthusiastically, 'Come see, Mommy and Daddy stuffed our stockings!'

The way he said it didn't quite sit right with Sally, though, again, she couldn't put her finger on why. She was still, after all, waking up. But something about this

Christmas morning felt different from the others, and not just because she was now old enough to know Santa Claus wasn't real.

It was that *smell*! It grew more and more powerful with every step, and paired with that gummed-up raspberry filling on Bill's face, it made Sally's stomach tumble and flip. Nothing she had encountered her whole live-long life had prepared her for something as strong—as unutterably revolting—as that smell.

But she trusted her big brother, and so she let him lead her farther into the sitting room, across the dirty carpet (Mommy would be *furious*!) and past the Christmas tree (which had gotten new decorations—what else had Billy done without her?) and to the blazing fireplace. She let him sit her down next to the hearth, nestled between the brick fireplace and the stacks of carefully wrapped presents. She let him carefully take her stocking down from its hook (another thing they usually did together) and place it reverently in her lap.

The smell was unbearable now. 'Bill, what—?'

'Close your eyes, Sal!'

Sal? Billy had never called his sister *Sal* before. But she squeezed her eyes tight—and her nose, lest she hurl and ruin the gifts in her stocking.

She listened to the fire crackle and pop as Bill took his own stocking and settled on the carpet beside her. And she noticed that the stocking in her lap was . . . *warm*.

'Bill, you made the fire too hot! Daddy'll get mad. This

stocking is practically all burned up!'

'It's fine, Sal, I promise!'

There it was again: *Sal.* Sally's tummy squirmed some more.

'Okay, open your eyes . . . *now!*'

That perennial Christmas delight shunted every concern from Sally's mind and she jolted her eyes open, beaming down excitedly at what lay in her lap.

It was . . . ropes?

'Come on, Sal, check 'em out!'

Bill was digging into his own stocking, and a wave of that *smell* crested over her and she shut her mouth, not daring to breathe.

Still, that trust she had for her big brother held firm, if not on its last strings.

And so, Sally dug her hands into her stocking, pushing through her own curious revulsion as she pushed through that weird, wet *warmth* and excavated it from her stocking—a pink, bedazzled sock made to look like a poodle, since she'd asked her parents every single year for a puppy.

Squishy, rubber tubes came spilling out into her lap, and a second, stronger wave of that queasy smell rushed up at her. Her eyes watered. What was she looking at? Her thoughts tumbled along with her stomach. The tubes were all connected in one long, never-ending rope, and it slid through her fingers like one of those liquid-filled toys Mommy sometimes let her get at Party City. She kept pulling and pulling and she almost giggled nervously—it was like those magician's hankies, except they were all pink. It was slick with something, something viscous and sticky that made her think of the raspberry filling all over Bill. It trembled and twitched in her hands, glistening in the firelight, and made a wet squelching sound. And it smelled . . .

It smelled like *poop*.

But still, that Christmas hope was hard to die. She glanced up, hesitantly hopeful, at Bill, who sat smiling at her in a way that scared her more than anything else.

'Bill . . . what is this? Is it . . .' She tried to brighten her smile and she gagged. 'Is it doggie toys? Did Mommy and Daddy finally get me a puppy?'

She looked down at what was in his lap, thinking maybe it would confirm her question—a doggie collar, a water bowl, doggy treats, maybe. But what she saw made very little sense to her.

In her brother's lap were four eyeballs.

'Mommy and Daddy *are* the gifts, Sal,' Bill said, his smile growing. 'Santa's *real*, Sal, and he came in the night to help me decorate.' As he spoke, he took four fish hooks from his stocking and meticulously pierced each eye on the tips to make little baubles. They hung from the metal hooks by the pink stalks attached to the backs of the eyeballs, swinging as he stood.

He turned to the tree to pick the perfect spot for the new ornaments, and as he did so Sally's eyes wandered up and around, truly taking in the room for the first time. The sunlight streaming in through the curtains had grown stronger, mixing its heat with that of the roaring fireplace. Garlands and streamers had magically gone up overnight, though they weren't the decorations Mommy put up every year. They were unrecognisable to Sally, weird bits of gooey stuff and streamers of thick cables and things that looked suspiciously like raw meat and picked-clean bones. Strung haphazardly over the Christmas tree were more of the slippery, ropey tubes, jouncing softly like the reins of Santa's reindeer sleigh.

And rising from it all was a thin caul of steam.

Sally sat there, frozen, her fingers numb in her lap, barely feeling the warm stickiness looped there in twitching coils. Billy's own stocking stuffers had spilled across the already-soiled carpet, and she saw now that they were dozens of teeth, thrown like jacks. Their roots were still attached, some bloody pink.

'Open this first!' Billy was standing over her, holding out a nicely wrapped gift he'd collected from beneath the tree. He placed it before her, then returned to his seat with his own similarly wrapped present.

Sally noticed something then that she'd missed before. As Bill had moved away, the Christmas tree came into view, and her eyes focused on its very tip. Usually Daddy placed a large, dazzling star there. In fact, she'd seen him do exactly this just weeks before. But for some reason the star was missing, and in its place . . .

Sally frowned. In its place sat the most peculiar thing. Her brain didn't know what to make of it. It looked like . . . well, she didn't know whether to giggle or scream at the thought of what it looked like.

Sitting atop the Christmas tree was a floppy piece of flesh that looked a bit like a chipolata sausage, but she was certain she'd seen it before. Yes, that one time Daddy had stepped out of the shower without realising the door was open. Now it was shrivelled and bloody and she hadn't even realised a penis was something her daddy could just take off whenever he wanted.

That was when everything caught up to her and Sally didn't know if she should cry, scream, or barf. She held it all in long enough to open the present—something about Big Bill's smile made her want to remain agreeable.

The gift was a box, meticulously wrapped in Frosty the Snow-Man paper and tied in a tinsel bow.

She slipped the bow from around the box and carefully found the seams in the paper. She split the tape at the bottom and folded the paper away. Usually she ripped and tore the paper away with just as her brother was doing, but just now she wanted to take her time.

Anything to postpone looking inside the box.

But when she finally did, she found her own mother staring up at her. With sightless, bloody sockets.

Sally screamed.

'*Merry Christmas, Sal!*'

Sally *screamed*.

I'LL BE HOME
FOR CHRISTMAS
A STORY
BY CARMILLA YUGOV

I don't know how long I've been on this journey.

The merciless Russian winter. Layers and layers of snow, the icy wind brushing against my face, almost razor sharp . . .

But I don't pay attention to any of that, not anymore.

I'm going home. All I want is to finally be home for Christmas.

This winter no longer bothers me. Neither does walking through the snow in my old, torn uniform. I know it will all be forgotten once I'm home.

I'm afraid.

What if . . .

No.

I haven't been home for years.

I brush the bad thoughts off. I have a feeling, a good feeling. Everything will be all right from now on. It's over. I'm going home.

Four years ago . . .

Memories will occasionally come back, and they'll haunt me. Our brains tend to forget the trauma, they push it away. But they come back, oh, they do.

Waking up screaming, as my friends kept silencing me, because we would have given our position away . . .

What happened to my friends?

I can't see their faces anymore. My mind has blocked them out too. I only see the blurry shapes where the human faces once had been. The bodies . . . I see what The Machine did to them. I see the open wounds, the severed limbs, the . . .

The faces have been erased. Машина, The Machine, has taken them away. Your identity? Doesn't matter any longer. The faces, almost human, but not quite. . . We're now the tiny parts of the machine. We can be replaced anytime. Like a screw. It broke and fell out? Put another one in and keep going. Your name? It means nothing.

I'm in pain.

And yet, I keep going.

My village is near. I can feel my heart beating faster.

I press the collar of my worn jacket against my cheeks, trying to protect my face from the wind. It makes my eyes teary. I wipe them with the back of my hand. I open my eyes again.

What if everything has been ruined?

The voice in my head is right. I look around. It's getting

dark, and I can't see too well. Or is it just the tears in my eyes? Are they really from the wind?

Try to remember

My house is up on the small hill, kind of secluded from the rest of the houses. I loved that hill. When I was a kid, I'd pull the small Christmas tree up the hill on my sleigh. The December winds never bothered me, because I knew I'd be warm and well once I was back inside.

why you're here.

I don't know what date it is. It could have been late Autumn when I started my journey, although I have no way of knowing how long it's really been. Our Christmas is on January 7th. What if I'm late?

I finally see the hill. My heart is jumping. I start to feel the tears in the back of my throat, but I swallow them.

You don't know what you'll find

The ruins everywhere. Have you looked around?

Climbing onto the hill now. From a distance, I see it.

The living room is illuminated, and I can see the smoke coming from the chimney. I smile. I start running through the snow, across the yard. And then I remember. I forgot about the Christmas tree! I run back to the sleigh and

There is no sleigh.

The house is still there, but the windows are broken. Is anyone there?

The front door has been removed, and from the inside, I see the empty hall.

My family, what happened to my family?

I was sixteen years old when I left home.

I hear a sound. Something bangs loudly, and it makes me jump. I start breathing faster, looking around. Something is happening?

It's just the snow that has fallen from the roof.

You've been jumpy since that night back in 1915.

Remember the grenade?

I don't want to remember. I'm home now, it doesn't matter

But it does. That grenade. Look down at your feet. Look around yourself.

No.

you lost both of your

The tears are clouding my eyes again.

I look down, defeated. I'm floating in the air. My legs are missing from the knees down.

that bang. and you were down on the ground, and they were gone and you were bleeding. your friends couldn't do anything, they

shut up

they carried you away, gave you something. Some drugs, to make it less painful?

SHUT UP

you kept talking, as huge drops of sweat slid down your face, and blood was pouring out. you became delirious. and there it was, your wish. you kept telling them you have to be home for Christmas, you can't die now, your family is there and they're waiting for you, you have to go back

266

I extend my arm, and reach out. My body shakes, but not from the cold. Ghosts can't feel the cold, can they? Sobs rip me from the inside. I'm screaming, but, even if my family was here, they wouldn't be able to hear me.

you never stopped searching for home

You died when you were seventeen. It's been four years. The war is long over. But you couldn't find peace until you were back.

The tears never stopped. I tried to move forward, but I couldn't.

I look behind me. I never left traces in the snow.

I look at the house once again. Close my eyes, try to remember it the way it once was, before . . .

before The Machine took over. and it took you with it

I'm still crying, but now the good memories are coming back. The happy days.

I extend my hand once again.

The wind is blowing harder, and it's colder, sharper than ever.

but it's done

I feel myself fading away, away with the wind. The memories are flooding over me. I force a faint smile, moments before it's all over.

I did it. I'm back home for Christmas.

AND END IT DOES NOT

A POEM
BY JOE CLEMENTS

What man was meant to live in such cold
and such dark?
What intoxicating sense of home
Leaves us indolent, static?
While sunk horizons weep for form
Once more.

Her islands hold their shores.
No figure seen
And each day ends
As dark
As next begins.
No withered leaves,
And each way darts
And bends
And leads me in.

If only we could see
As the trees
Of worlds born and razed

In seeming instance.

Condensed to screaming infants
By neglectful gaze
Hope reflected rays
When once they were.

Now a light sweeps the cabin,
Blinding.
Surely simple filament
And low wattage
Shouldn't sear the iris as this?

Still unclean
With wayside values
The bed delves valleys
Alluring once, til headward feathers
Gather
Saturating lonely end.

Once so easily traversed,
The landscape rolls in endless
Vague and creeping horror.

And I should be the first
Should no soul other feel the Cosmic drag.
Like perched on windy mountain crag
In the basement of the world.

HUNGRY

AN ILLUSTRATION
TO ACCOMPANY
'EVERY HUNT IS A COLD ONE'
BY MARCUS HAWKE

'Despite its size, the bear was sickly. Thin. Weak and hungry. His bones showed through the patchy white fur that was pink in some places from having fallen out.

The skin around one eye hung loose in the socket, and the eyeball along with it. And there, wetting the nose, was a stain of red. The snout dripped with it . . . '

THE CRUEL HEAT

A SEQUEL TO
'THE VIOLENT SNOW'
BY PATRICK WHITEHURST

Ray Jones felt a breath of cool air wash over his face. He sat upright and wiped the sleep from his eyes. She'd turned the air conditioner on again. The couch cushions felt cool to the touch. The atmosphere like a morgue despite the feverish temperatures outside.

He groaned, got to his feet, and went across the living room to the panel, rubbing the ache in his lower back. The display read seventy degrees. Far too cold. Tapping the console, he shut down the system and reset it for eighty-five Fahrenheit.

His wife peeked over his shoulder. 'You have got to be kidding me, Ray.'

'Too cold in here.'

Agatha Jones rolled her eyes. She plucked the floral print gardening gloves from her fingers and stomped off toward the kitchen, muttering about the heat wave. It may have been a week to Christmas, but it felt more like an oven outside than a snow globe. While her husband napped, she'd been sweating in her small garden, doing what she could with her beloved plants in the uncertain weather. After cleaning her brother's meat packing offices all morning, she deserved the break.

Ray smelled earthy soil in her wake, not to mention a bit of sweat. He was sure the chilly air felt good on her skin. To him it served as a reminder of something he never again wanted to think about.

He followed her into the kitchen, rubbing the sleep from his eyes. Since he'd returned from Flagstaff, he'd been a nervous wreck. She had to have noticed. For two weeks he'd been having nightmares, seeing those icy creatures whenever he shut his eyes. He could feel their paralyzing touch with every beat of his heart and could barely consider their origins without fearing for his own sanity.

He'd not told Agatha about the attack at Number Twelve Pine Lane. How could he? No one, not even his wife, would believe such a tale. Though proof of his horrific *hermication*, his alone time up north, cawed at him from the top of the fridge. The raven was just another reminder to Ray, but one he wouldn't want to be without.

'Quiet, bird,' Agatha said.

Ray poured cold coffee into a freshly scrubbed Jones Plumbing and Cooling mug. He grabbed a peanut from the cupboards and handed it off to the large black bird. Herbert, as Ray named him in the cabin, happily snatched the treat and flew off into the living room to land on the fireplace near the Christmas tree. Ray sipped his coffee and waited for Agatha to say something. He knew she would. They'd been married long enough for him to understand her body language.

She continued to scrub the soil from her fingers when she spoke. 'First off, Ray. You're going to have to do something about that damn bird. I try to keep a clean place here for the kids and that bird shits everywhere.'

Keeping the bird, Ray said to himself.

'Secondly, you're going to call your dad tonight. Tell him you're sorry. Tell him you were feeling stressed out by life or something, I don't know. Just get your job back.'

Ray looked at the mug. His wife's orange-scented soap filled his nostrils. Face the situation, he thought. Will do.

'We're burning through the savings, you know. If you don't start bringing money in soon, we'll dip into the college fund, or we'll sell the cabin in Flagstaff. And I don't plan to work a second job forever.'

Oh, I'm selling it, Ray said to himself. No way in hell will I step foot back in the place. It's going as is too. A wreck.

After his encounter with the creatures, Ray boarded up the place and drove his ass back to Phoenix as quick as the snowy roads allowed. In their murderous frenzy, the icy beasts had done a bang-up job on his home away from home. The place felt like a coffin to him now, full of sick memories.

'And then there's that thing on the mantel. That 3-D model you protect like it was a holy relic. I know things

275

weren't perfect before, Ray. Trust me. But you need to pull yourself together. What is that thing anyway?'

That thing, he thought, is how I planned to apologize to dad.

Only he couldn't do it. He couldn't bring himself to gift destruction to his own father, no matter how much of a dick the old man could be. The larynx, which he'd placed carefully on the mantel when he'd arrived home, and warned no one to touch, would bring too much destruction and pain. To use it called forth the creatures from whatever dimensional graveyard they inhabited. That agony, Ray had come to realize, he wished on no one.

'It's nothing, Aggy. Just a gift from Chuck. Makes a weird sound when you blow in it, that's all. I'll get rid of it before one of the kids gets their hands on it.'

Agatha turned from the sink and faced the living room. The sparkling white lights on the Christmas tree reflected off the window, despite the bright sunshine streaming through the glass. She nodded at one of the girls in the living room. Ray followed her gaze.

'A bit late for that, hon.'

Ray's scream made both Agatha and Herbert jump. His youngest, Robin, pulled the larynx from her lips after having puffed through it, a shocked look on her chubby, freckled face. His Jones Plumbing and Cooling mug shattered on the hardwood floors. Robin made a retching sound and dropped the blue plastic model at her feet, where it broke into three pieces. A chilled terror washed over him. Even Agatha shook her head, as if to wake herself from a bad trip.

'Shit, Ray,' she said. 'Suddenly got sick to my stomach. What just happened? You dropped your . . . '

Before he could answer, Ray found himself in the living room. He snatched the pieces of the larynx off the floor. A single thought ran through his mind as he stuffed them into his sweatpants.

Should have destroyed it. Should have destroyed it.

The raven launched off the mantel and started circling the living room. Robin ducked under its wide black wings and ran from the room, choking back sobs. Agatha chased after her, telling their youngest everything was okay. Dad was just in a mood, she said, and that always got the new pet riled. To calm her, Aggy suggested they put a Christmas movie on in the den.

Ray ignored them. He went to the front window and peered into the yard. Waves of heat shimmered off the concrete, gravel, and asphalt. Herbert flapped over to perch on his shoulder, his black eyes staring intently onto the street. Both went to the back of the house and checked there. Lizards and ants crawled around in the freshly turned dirt. Nothing more.

'What do you see, Herbert?' Ray asked the raven. It croaked quietly. 'Maybe it's too hot for them.' He could feel the heat through the glass. The backdoor. Aggy hadn't closed it all the way when she came in, had she? A gap of a few inches, not much, but anything could barge in. Ray went to the door with Herbert clinging to his shoulder.

Freezing air washed over his forearm. He slammed the door and slid the locking bolt. The hair on his arm pricked up from the draft, but quickly settled. His heart pounded. Sweat formed on his forehead. The unseasonable weather didn't help. That weather he once hated, but now loved.

'Maybe the heat is keeping them away, Herbert.' His voice trembled. That night flashed in his mind. The icy claw reaching for his throat.

Ray went to the kitchen. Beneath the sink he found his arsenal. A pack of lighters and three hairspray cans. He collected one of each and started a harried patrol through the house. Checking first the kids and Aggy. All three now sat lazily in the den watching the opening scenes of a Grinch movie. He remembered, as he stalked his prey, that his wife planned to make Snickerdoodles later. His daughters ignored him, Robin's trauma already forgotten, but Ray felt Aggy's eyes bore into his back.

Half an hour passed with no sign. The 3-D printed larynx may have summoned the creatures, but Phoenix kept them at bay. Too hot for the bastards, Ray mused.

Again, as he set the tools of their destruction upon the mantel and within easy reach, he practiced his newfound calming techniques. Slow the shakes, ebb the tide of fear, and stare at the ceiling. Deep breaths. Deep breaths. Clammy, sour-smelling sweat covered him.

Satisfied the imminent threat had passed, Herbert returned to his perch atop the fridge. He ruffled his dark feathers and turned a wary eye on Ray. Then closed them for a nap.

'Better clean up this coffee and go watch the movie. Play it cool,' Ray muttered.

Later, while his eyes stared at the flat screen, he saw only his daughter's lips pressed to the cursed larynx. Should have destroyed it. When the movie ended and they went to bed, he paid no attention to the kids, nor his wife, and slid under the blankets wracked with tension. He made sure the thermostat remained in the eighties.

He stared at the ceiling, noting the spin of the fan above his head. His breathing improved and his eyes started to blur with the blissful arrival of sleep, but there was something there. Some *thing* above him. Smoke? Something on fire? The wispy form moved with purpose but faded in and out of view.

He focused, becoming more alert, and got a better glimpse. The veins in his neck bulged. There was one in the house. Ray fumbled with his bedding and fell to the floor. Next to him, Agatha mumbled in her sleep and rolled over.

Ray jumped to his feet in only his white boxer shorts. His round belly, dripping with cold perspiration, hung over the elastic band. It had been there, of that he was certain, but where was it now?

He searched the room, seeing nothing, but couldn't forget the image. Like a puff of steam that formed into a tiny head with a round mouth. No other features. No eyes, no nose, or ears, just that mouth. As he searched near the bathroom door, he felt a wave of coldness. Turning, Ray caught another glimpse of the towering creature before it evaporated.

The thought crossed his mind as it had earlier. Too hot for the bastards. His daughter. She'd called one forth, but it couldn't materialize in the heat. It wanted to. Oh, did it want to. But it could only materialize so far.

'Wherever you're coming from must be cold as the Antarctic.' Ray made his way downstairs and wondered if the creature would follow. He raised the temperature in the house and then walked lightly to the kitchen. He had an idea. Something to prove his theory, and he hoped it wasn't a stupid one.

Herbert gurgled to him when he entered, his stare alert and curious. Ray figured he sensed the other presence. Hoped he'd help if needed should things go south. Just as he had in Flagstaff.

He stopped at the fridge, sighed heavily, and swung open the freezer door.

At first nothing happened. Chilled air wafted out. Ray felt the coolness against his face and bare chest. Herbert watched him with mild curiosity, unsure of Ray's intentions. The raven ruffled his feathers as he too felt the chill.

For the briefest moment Ray spied movement in front of him. That moving wisp of steam, which trembled and glittered in the weak lighting, began to form into a clawed hand. Jesus, it's here. It's not just my mind, he thought. It's *really* here.

Larger than his damn head. Fingers like the talons of a hulking eagle. It crystalized from the air itself, icy blue, deadly, and determined. It swiped at him, nearly gutting his belly, before Ray slammed the freezer closed. For a moment it continued to slash, seeking meat, before it melted. Drops of water fell from the icy hand and soon became nothing more than a puddle on the floor.

Herbert cocked his head.

'It's not gone. It's still here waiting for me. For the girls.'

He spent the rest of the night thinking. His feet on the coffee table, snores coming from the bedroom, he thought of the invisible, ethereal ghoul clawing at his brains this moment, unable to score the kill.

By sunrise he had an idea.

Chuck, he texted, *I know you're still in a coma, but I want you to know. Another one is here in the Phoenix house. Robin used the larynx. She blew through it. I'm going to have to kill the thing if I can.*

A pinkish hue began to fill the night air. Snores rumbled meekly from behind the closed doors upstairs. Ray, now dressed in a green flannel and grey sweatpants, readied his hair spray and lighter before he opened the freezer door again. He placed his phone on the counter, which he'd set to record, and readied himself as it filmed. The camera caught the view of his back, as he faced the open freezer, which he'd set to the coldest temp. Herbert sat above the appliance, watching curiously. Curls of icy air formed in front of him, but he saw no sign of the icy creature.

The phone kept recording for what seemed an eternity. He finally turned it off. Nothing happened. Had the creature gone? Herbert gurgled and Ray sighed, letting some of the tension deflate from his shoulders.

That's when he felt the heat at his back.

Sensing a threat, the raven cawed frantically and swooped to his shoulder, eyes alert to the blazing heat in the room. He landed on Ray, and they turned to face the source of the heat. Ray's eyes widened with terror.

The air sparked. Static electricity formed from the oxygen itself. Glowing embers zipped around his face. The fireworks began to coalesce, forming into a shape. A large, thin creature made of blue flames and glowing red embers shimmered into being. The stink of burned toast filled the room. Ray choked on the smoke and stumbled back. Herbert flapped his wings to fan the smoke, though it did little good. The fiery monster turned its head toward Ray. There were no discernible eyes that Ray could see, no nose . . . like one of the ice creatures. Only this apparition seemed made of fire and heat. When it turned toward him, he realized his mistake. The creature seemed to be missing a hand. The very hand he'd melted in front of the freezer.

This wasn't a different being at all, but the same monster.

Ray stammered. 'Supposed to be made of ice. How could you . . . how could you change?'

But what did he really know at all when it came to these beasts? What did Chuck for the matter? What did anyone?

It struck him in a quick, burning blow to the chest. Ray felt an icy dread wash over him, erasing the pain of the singed clothing that burned against his chest, and he felt himself flown into the cupboards. The wood panelling cracked when he hit it.

Herbert took flight, landing atop the fridge, and Ray fell to the ground. Contact with the fiery beast paralyzed him with fear. Just as it had in Flagstaff. He'd been burned, perhaps badly, but felt only that cold, hollow fear from head to toe. The hair spray can rolled around on the floor, a useless reminder that he understood nothing of these creatures.

Blue flames licked at the kitchen ceiling from the tip of its small head as the horror stumbled awkwardly away from him. Splayed feet spit embers as it walked toward the dining room, intent to move deeper into the house. It's footsteps left small fires of burning linoleum in its wake.

Ray could only watch, paralyzed, as it stalked his family. They were upstairs, still dreaming dreams of Santa and candy canes, and he could not move. He could do nothing to save them.

What a fool he'd been.

WELCOME DECEMBER

A STORY
BY MONA KABBANI

She has red hair. That's what really drew Malory in. Red hair and a name like a fairytale. Allison. *Al-is-son.* Like Alice in Wonderland but without the extra commitment. She has red hair and a smile that could make sunflowers grow in the dark.

Malory swipes through the pictures of Allison on her tablet. Her Victorian black bed consumes her bum and toes as she shifts about, cradled around her device, incense of white sage and cinnamon traversing across the room to her senses. She runs her fingers through her black hair and wonders what she'd look like if she could manage to dye such dark strands red. If she could turn her own hair to flame.

No, she thinks. She much prefers the colour on Allison.

Christmas lights twinkle about her red walls and Malory taps on the profile's private messages.

M: *Northwest corner of Greenwood Cemetery, right?*

A: *That would be correct! I can't wait to see you there.*

Malory bites her lip and smiles. She sets the tablet down and slides off her bed. Smoke trails her as she walks over to her large wooden vanity. Its mirror reflects her excitement.

This will be a first for her and she has no idea why she's waited this long. Near to having never come close.

She grabs the black sweater and plaid skirt from off her chair, slides the clothing over her skin, and bounces slightly on the balls of her feet, shaking off nerves.

No sweat. You got this.

On the counter of her vanity is a knife. An archaic one that once belonged to user *Gorelord42ox* from eBay but is now hers for the *low* price of seventy-two dollars and sixty cents and the diminishment of her pride from begging for that price drop. She picks it up, swirls it in the air, lines the curve of its blade around her wrist, but does not dare slice. Instead, she pulls a ribbon from out of her drawer and wraps a big red bow around its wooden handle. She sheaths it in bubble wrap—*not special, but it will have to do*— and slides it between her inner calf and high sock.

She gives herself one last look in the mirror. A skull at the base of the glass stares up at her and she turns to it with a grin.

'It'll be all right, Hamlet. I won't fuck this up. It'll be all right.'

Hamlet doesn't respond. But she can read his answer in his empty eye sockets. The repeated reassurance.

You've got this.

She leans down and kisses him on the top of his head. Red lips leave their stain, superimposed on alternating layers of red and black against bone. She chuckles, grabs a jacket, and skips out the door.

The air outside is frigid, snow dusting the sidewalks and now dusting her body. She hops, nearly trips, and regains her balance, a miniature avalanching falling from her shoulder.

It's 3:00 AM but the street is filled with light. Swirls of red and green and neon snowflakes arched between telephone poles. Snowmen and reindeer with fluorescent binds crowd in front of the town movie theatre like they just can't wait to get inside. She walks past the theatre's dim windows, thinking about Allison behind the counter, her bright red nails handing guests overfilled bags of popcorn.

The second Malory spotted her, she knew she was the one.

She'd bought a ticket, hesitated before the concession stand, but couldn't bring herself to say hello. She watched the flick; seven dollars and fifty cents wasted.

Or so she thought.

Because Allison found her anyway.

A: *It's instant. It only takes one glance to know someone is right for you. Compatible. You walking by was all I needed.*

M: *I'm glad it was worth it. That movie was awful.*

A: *You're funny. I'm glad, too.*

Allison helped her throw out all remnants of her past

self. All the bits of her that were weighing her down like rusty anchors. The crosses and the photographs and the letters of yore. She didn't even need to be present. To be in Malory's room with her to encourage her internal exodus. A lending hand reaching out through a digital screen, melting away her limits.

And now, Malory floats.

A crow croaks. The streets have little activity. Only those in the know bustle about. Most of the townspeople are still in bed, waiting until next week to stir in their homes, Santa hats on their nightstands collecting dust as their children vibrate in wait.

A: *Our celebration will be better. A true welcoming of spirit.*

Malory has yet to meet Allison face to face. This will be a first for them. But Malory knows Allison is always close. Always with her in her mind. She knows this by the way she bites into a vanilla ice cream cone freshly handed to her over the creamery counter and its centre bleeds. How her heels squelch when she slides her toes into her boots only to reveal rubber soles when she checks for what made the sound. The way her chest jolts her awake in the middle of the night, her skin drenched in sweat and her thoughts alight with red hair and gore.

Al-is-son.

She passes the town diner. Passes the booth she sat in a week ago with her visiting mother as she divulged her truth. Divulged how all her crosses were now gone, defecated on a pile of steaming rot somewhere far, far away. How her mother's face scrunched in disgust, an angry mouth telling her to just stay in this god-awful place agape with sin.

She tried to explain who was the one to ruin who in the first place. But her mother would hear none of it.

And her mother was one of the final anchors to be dropped.

Are you close?

She can hear Allison's voice in her head. A tickling whisper, so pleasant yet so invading. She wonders if she can respond,

I'm near,

but she receives no answer in return. The digital screen in her mind seems to only go one way. At least for now, she hopes.

It's no matter. The destination is in her sight. She picks up the pace, feeling the knife rub against her skin, tease its tearing. Her mind is too filled with flame to notice and the crows mask the creak of her skin. She nearly slips, a sheet of thin ice shoving her trotting feet to the side, but regains her balance and leaps onto the grass.

She's here.

But she does not see Allison.

She slips the knife out from her sock and holds it behind her back, ambling about the gravestones and weeds. Everything is coated in ice. Everything is frost.

The northwest corner, she remembers.

Come to me.

What leaves are left in nearby trees shudder and crickets chirp. Crows croak. She wants to whistle as she moves but knows the sound would only disturb the silence.

Alert the unknown.

A breeze passes under her nostrils.

She follows her senses. She can smell the smoke. She sees the tree and then sees the flame. Allison's red hair.

Al-is-son.

Her feet move faster until they are a mere casket apart. And then she stops.

Allison approaches her step by step, her body adorned in a black robe, her arms holding a present. A medium-sized crimson box with a fat green bow. The girl smiles and Malory smiles back at the most beautiful person she's ever seen, fidgeting with the knife against her spine.

'I knew you'd come,' Allison says. She lifts the box slightly as if in offering to Malory. But Malory knows better. 'I could feel you the whole time.'

This present is for her in other ways.

'Of course I'd come.'

'Did you bring it?'

Malory reveals the knife from behind her back. Allison looks at it questioningly and Malory meets her stare, realizing the bubble wrap still clings to the blade. She scrambles to remove it and shoves the wrapping in her coat pocket then laughs nervously and stands tall to redeem herself. Allison giggles and Malory relaxes.

'Come, come,' the redhead beckons, and they both turn to the side where the festivities are held.

Malory steps up to the circle as one member breaks it to drop a fresh robe across her shoulders. She nods in thanks and slips her arms through the sleeves. Allison glances at her and both girls grin in unison, Allison setting the present down on the grass in front of them as they lift their hoods on up over their heads. The chanting still penetrates through the thick fabric, words that translate in Allison's mind and seep into her own. Malory sets the knife across her lap.

Free me.

The tree before them is on fire but it does not burn. Its pines are eternal and it is, in fact, the tree that consumes the fire. Snow still rests on the needles within the flame.

Feed me.

Allison scooches herself and the present forward toward the tree and Malory follows suit. The circle closes behind them as members adjust into a tighter line.

Bleed with me.

They are a breath away from the trunk. Malory hesitates, staring at the palette of knobs that nearly forms a face, unsure of how she's expected to get inside. Allison reaches over and squeezes Malory's thigh, egging her on. Malory's grip trembles around the knife's handle. But she can feel Allison in her head, reassuring her, *you'll do just fine.*

Be with me.

Do it.

Malory arches the blade over her shoulder, grunts, and drives it into the tree. The tree hisses and groans like it's releasing pent-up steam. Decades worth. With all her strength, Malory drags the blade down, cutting a slit into the trunk that opens up like a zipper. The smell of burning cinnamon escapes from the wound and so does a thick, purple tongue.

You're doing just fine.

The tongue is the size of her torso and it thrashes about like a worm out of soil. It punches against the frosted dirt, nearly licking at Malory's knees. Allison quickly grabs for Malory's hands, takes the blade, and slices down her palm. Malory winces but isn't shocked for long, transfixed by the crimson red that leaks down her wrists into the snow below.

Don't lose focus.

Allison slides the present over to her and Malory lifts its lid. She dips her wounded hand in and wraps her fingers around the gift. Out comes a thumping heart the size of her palm, beating twice as fast as what's in her own chest. It makes her hyper-aware of her own senses, slow and dense and lethargic, and she sinks a bit into nausea.

'You're doing just fine,' but this time, Allison says it aloud.

Despite the weakness in her belly, Malory furrows her brow in determination and shoves her hand into the wound above the tongue. The tongue senses and retracts, disappearing back into its home. Malory feels the soft flesh of wood against her knuckles, the thick muscle running across her fingers like she is a xylophone made up of bones. The tongue finds purchase under her fingernails, lifts, and opens her hand for her, relieving her of the weight she carries.

The heart disappears down its gullet, the thumping silenced, and Malory's fingers are suspended in nothingness.

'Pull your hand out,' Allison whispers.

The tongue runs across Malory's wound, lapping at her existence. Soothing her strain.

Yes. You're doing just fine.

'Malory.'

Malory's mind gets lost in the feeling. The sensation enveloping her skin, tingling her senses. That fat, purple tongue caressing her, making her feel so warm and so safe.

'Malory!'

Malory is yanked back. Wrenched away from that nothingness, the soothing connection torn in half. She screams, missing the touch of those taste buds on her as her arm rips from the trunk. She wants to yell at Allison. To beg her why she broke the connection? Why she would remove her in the exact moment she was finally doing so well?

But then a crunch answers her fury.

Blood bursts from the slit in the trunk and rains on them like a massacre. The slit seals with that crunch and some of its excrement landed in Malory's mouth so that she has to cough to unclog it from her throat.

The fire disappears, absorbed by the pines. The tree is no longer a demon but just a tree, quiet and still. The circle does the same, disappearing into the ethereal. Malory falls back against the frosted dirt and looks up at the sky. The crows no longer croak and the blood has begun to freeze, tightening her skin. Allison comes into frame, a vision of gore backdropped by the black night. Her hair cascades across Malory's chest and Malory wonders what it would be like for the flames to lap at her bones.

You did so well.

Thank you.

Allison leans in. Malory shuts her eyes as their lips press, the transfer of blood lighting the butterflies in her chest aflame, the sizzling in Allison's skull igniting in her own. Their connection is now eternal, their pact solidified. The digital screen no longer goes one way.

Thank you eternally.

Allison pulls away and giggles. Malory's lips curl in tandem with the flight of her joy. They both escalate until they climax into a laughter that slices through the cinnamon air.

Everything is silent. Everything is at peace.

Welcome, welcome, welcome December.

AUTHOR PROFILES

AFTERWORD

BY CHRISTOPHER BADCOCK

AUTHOR OF "THOSE YOU KILLED" AND "EVERYONE TO THE TABLE"

It's a wonderful contradiction; winter. A season that can be depressing, with its early nights, hazardous ice, and *bitter chills.* Even Christmas, for some, only amplifies a loneliness felt throughout the year, or the stress of meeting expectations.

Blimey, is the afterword really going to be this morose?

Let's flip to the other side of this coin. The majesty of it all. The colours you find on the tree, and adorning decked halls. Snow gently falling, the sort that enchants hearts both young and old, and the flurries that leave behind white hills screaming for the tread of a sledge or two.

The gifts. The reactions to those gifts.

The religious stories that, atheist or faithful, can bring with them a sense of wonder, of wisdom, and hope.

And the food. *Chef's kiss.*

Where am I going with this? Honestly, I have no idea.

When Nick Harper asked me to write the afterword for

this revised and illustrated edition of Bitter Chills, I was thrilled, honoured, and completely flummoxed. How do you round off a collection of brilliant tales written by some of the most exciting voices in the indie horror community right now?

How?!

I've never written an afterword, just an acknowledgement. Do I try to be deep and meaningful, as above? And risk sounding like a pompous a-hole, as above. Do I simply shower well-deserved praise on the authors and a tonne of thanks to you, the intrepid reader who spent hard-earned money on this tome? Or maybe a whistle-stop tour of Christmas horror? Those things are always interesting, right?

What even is an afterword? That all-knowing being we call Google tells me that it's "*the concluding section in a book, after the main story*".

Helpful!

I think the safest bet might be to just cover all of the above, loose every arrow and hope that at least one of them impales you.

Let's delve into the history of yuletide spookiness for a moment.

Now, this is by no means an exhaustive trip, I knew a little about this stuff, and I've dug a little more to try and give you something beyond my own rambling. I'd encourage any who're interested though, to jump down this rabbit hole if you ever find the time. Some of the points I mention below could occupy you for days, as we move further back through time you'll find pieces that have kept scholars busy for entire lifetimes. If, however, you're like me, and just want to sound cool and knowledgeable at some Christmas gathering, what follows should be sufficient ammunition, providing you don't come across the festive equivalent of Matt Damon's *Good Will Hunting*.

Let's begin in Victorian Britain; a time and place that has become synonymous with Christmas, thanks in the most part to a certain Mr Dickens.

Many see Charlie D (yes, that's what I'm calling him) as the harbinger of what might be considered Christmas horror, and they'd be right, sort of. He arguably revived a long-lost tradition with *A Christmas Carol*, and reminded the British public—from the great unwashed to the height of aristocracy—of the good ol' days of Christmases of yore. Suddenly, horror was back in the mainstream, at least at Christmas, anyway. It was 1843.

Twenty-three years before this though, Washington Irving—author of *The Legend of Sleepy Hollow*—released a series of stories entitled *The Sketch Book of Geoffrey Crayon, Gent*. Nestled within this collection is a little gem known as *The Christmas Dinner*, a story that sees the residents of Bracebridge Hall exchange stories of goblins and ghosts on Christmas Eve. If you've never read this mostly-forgotten classic, search it out this December, snuggle up with a blanket and your hot brew of choice, dim those lights, and enjoy. It's delightfully dark, and something that Susan Hill would echo in the opening of *The Woman in Black* almost 150 years later.

Irving hasn't gotten us there yet though, so let's step back a few more centuries.

It's 1623 and William Shakespeare releases *The Winter's Tale*, a sad story of sprites and goblins best read during the winter months. But as much as Bill was a literary trailblazer, in this instance he too was inspired by what had come before him. Thirty-four years before the bard dipped his quill, Christopher Marlowe wrote of winter ghosts and spirits in *The Jew of Malta*. Marlowe is certainly a dude worth learning more about; the poet, brawler, duellist, magician, womaniser, and spy, met an untimely end at a young age; his death is still shrouded in mystery, but had he lived a longer life, his name might've been as widely known as Shakespeare's.

During this same period, across the Atlantic pond, ancient traditions long observed by the native Americans were being lost through colonization. Among them, the Passamaquoddy tales of frost giants; characters that can also be found in Old Norse mythology dating back even further, to a time when Christmas was known as Sol Invictus, Midwinter, Solstice, Saturnalia and Yule, and was celebrated on December 21st. It's from these old legends that Roxie Voorhees carved out her own tale that can be found within these pages, which happens to be one of my favourites in this collection.

So where do we end? Or rather, where does it begin? Those Norse legends are certainly old, they existed as oral tales for who knows how long, but they weren't written down until the 13th century, when Snorri Sturluson (I'm basically picturing *Gimli* from *Lord of the Rings*) composed the Prose Edda and Poetic Edda. Is it him? Is he the Father of Christmas horror? He's got the name for it, and he absolutely had a massive beard; I refuse to believe otherwise.

He probably wasn't the first to write about such things, though.

In fact, we don't really know who was. We can venture back a few hundred years more and find the Sagas of the Icelanders (an epic title if ever I've heard one), a vast collection of tales from Iceland, written between the 9th and 11th centuries. These anonymous stories deal with a multitude of subjects, but include wintery tales of ghosts and gods, and even zombies! Could *this* ancient text be the first ever example of recorded winter horror?

Perhaps.

Or perhaps not.

Nobody really knows.

There were probably oral tales before this, spoken and never written, lost to the wind, and time.

Isn't that quite fitting though? After all, we often find horror in uncertainty, scares in the sketchy nature of things, fear in what we don't understand.

Many of the stories in this collection play with this

very idea, the uneasiness we feel when we don't really know what's going on, and it's a fine line to tread. The area of ambiguity is a slither between frustration and perfection, I think each of the authors in here who set their stall in this region, executed magnificently.

This brings me nicely to that final point (it's like I planned it). The authors. These talented humans aren't just great writers, they're lovely people too. I've been a part of the Blood Rites Writers' Circle for a while now, and I can safely say these weirdos are some of the nicest people I've ever met. Friendly, supportive, funny, genuine, Nerds.

It isn't like it once was; the road to publication, it's arguably more difficult now than it ever has been. Indie authors have to work extra hard to break through the noise of well-established figures, content shared online is curated—mostly—with the aim of higher engagement, the more likes, the more comments, the better. I've seen it myself on my own social spaces, where a photo of a book written by Stephen King thirty years ago gets ten times more engagement than a post about an exciting new author with a unique voice. To thrive in this environment, to get your book in the hands of as many people as possible, an indie author requires nothing less than unrelenting determination. The writers featured in this book have that, and they deserve all the exposure they get. If you can, please take the time to follow each of them, some have novels—myself included—and some are featured in other collections, buy those books, if your bank account allows it. Being attached to a multi-million dollar publisher isn't always a sign of a great writer, take a chance on someone you've never heard of, someone working their day job, maybe even night shifts too, whilst caring for their family, balancing bills and life, and chasing their dream of becoming an author. You never know, you might just find your new favourite writer.

If you're reading this, you're already doing it, taking that chance on a group of unknowns, keep at it, I can't stress enough how much it means. Thank you, from me, Nick Harper and all of the authors involved in this wonderful collection.

Thank you.

Christopher Badcock
author of *Those You Killed*
5th July 2021

ACKNOWLEDGEMENTS

Thank you to all the readers and writers who have supported Blood Rites Horror since *Bitter Chills* and stuck with us through the lows and highs of our publishing journey so far.

Thank you, especially, to all the authors in this book, who not only contributed those original stories that would inspire my faith in this press and its mission, but put so much time and work into making this second edition truly special.

Thank you to the *Abominable Book Club* for taking a leap on this book, and to all the readers who might discover us as a result of that.

And thank you to my partner, without whom I'd have gone mad a long time ago.

DENVER GRENELL

Denver Grenell is a writer of horror & dark fiction who lives with his family in a small rural town in New Zealand. A life-long horror hound who got back into writing after a long break, he is now making up for lost time, furiously expelling every idea that has collected inside his skull over the years.

His stories have been featured in various anthologies from Crystal Lake Publishing, Black Hare Press, Blood Rites Horror as well as on Hawk & Cleaver's *The Other Stories* podcast. His debut collection of short stories *The Burning Boy & Other Stories* is out now through Beware The Moon Publishing.

Signup to his newsletter and find short stories/reviews and miscellaneous debris at **www.bewarethemoon.co.nz**.

KYLE J. DURRANT

Kyle J. Durrant was born in 1997 and raised in East Anglia, though has probably spent most of his life exploring fantasy universes and macabre realities. He fell in love with writing when he was ten, and hasn't stopped since.

When not writing, he tends to sit in varying stages of existential dread, or delves into video games, books, and movies. He has written copious amounts of notes, which drastically outnumber his completed stories.

To find more of Kyle's work, and keep up to date with his writing, follow him on Instagram (**@kylejdurrantauthor**). Kyle's first collection of cosmic horror and weird fiction, *Beyond Dimensional Veils*, is available now on Amazon.

ROXIE
VOORHEES

Roxie Voorhees (she/her) is a tangled threesome of *Gag Me With a Spoon, Welcome to the Darkside,* and *Catch Me Outside.* Originally from California, she now resides with her mastador, Bellatrix, in Indiana, where she refuses to use the word *pop*, is hella progressive, and dreams of a proper taco.

You can have your heart broken in her upcoming story "Cuca Vai te Pegar" in Dark Dispatch's *The Dead Inside* (edited by Laurel Hightower and Sandra Ruttan), and find her co-editing Camp Horror (with a foreword by Eric LaRocca, author of *Things Have Gotten Worse Since We Last Spoke*) with Spencer Hamilton, author of *The Fear.* She is currently working on her debut novel, *Beneath the Tule of the Valley.*

SPENCER HAMILTON

Spencer Hamilton is an LGBTQIA+ horror author based in Philadelphia. His debut collection and novel, *Kitchen Sink* and *The Fear*, were both published in 2020.

This year he launched a new series with *Welcome to Smileyland*—which is free to download at **www.SpencerHamiltonBooks.com**—and his latest release, the novella *Sister Funtime*. His next novel, *Hive*, releases in 2022.

Spencer has been a mainstay at Blood Rites Horror since the beginning. His *Kitchen Sink* story "A Rebellion in Words" was reprinted in the very first issue of *SPINE* magazine, the second issue of which saw the birth of Smileyland with his mini comic "Smile, It's Halloween!" (in collaboration with Nick Harper).

In addition to *Bitter Chills*, Spencer's fiction has featured in *Parasite Gods* ("I Will Devour You", winner of the *Parasite*

Gods flash fiction contest), *Wild Violence*, *Welcome to the Funhouse*, and *Pulp Harvest*.

He contributed a writing prompt to Nick Harper's *Exorcises*, and he is co-editing the upcoming anthology *Camp Horror* with Roxie Voorhees.

CARLA
ELIOT

Carla is a UK writer of horror, supernatural thrillers, and dark fiction. Her work often encompasses an underlying message and frequently dives into the paranormal.

Four of Carla's short stories feature in anthologies by Blood Rites Publishing. Her work has also been published by Quill & Crow Publishing House, Black Hare Press, Ghost Orchid Press, Night Terror Novels, and Jazz House Publications. To find out more about Carla and her writing, visit **carlaeliot.com** or search for **@writecarla** on Instagram and Twitter.

CASS
OAKLEY

Cass is a born and bred yam yam with a love of all things ghastly and gruesome. Having been an aspiring writer since she was in her single-digit years, it took procrastination from a fiddly classics postgrad to cement her tales onto paper.

An avid film, book, and game fan, Cass can often be found absorbed in other worlds—but usually in the Black Country with her array of pets. She finds writing about herself in third person incredibly unnerving.

Her other work can be found in the short story anthology *Parasite Gods*, and buried deeply in folders on her computer.

You can stalk her on Instagram **@cass_wba.**

CHRISTOPHER BADCOCK

Christopher works as a Marketing Consultant by day, and by night pursues his passion for writing. His debut novel, *Those You Killed*, was published through Blood Rites Horror in April 2021 and has garnered rave reviews from readers across the world. Available in eBook, paperback and hardback form from Barnes & Noble, Book Depository, Waterstones, Amazon and many others. Keep your eyes (ears) open for the audiobook, available on iTunes and Audible in 2022.

He lives in Nottingham, United Kingdom, with his four-year-old daughter, Aubriella, and is currently working on a much-delayed collection of short stories entitled *Iniquities*. Hopefully it'll see the light of day in 2022. Beyond that, you can expect to see his second novel, apocalyptic dark satire *Finale*, in 2023.

CARMILLA YUGOV

Carmilla was born in 1998. As a kid, she enjoyed watching characters like Hannibal Lecter and Van Helsing on TV (without her parents' permission). In her early teens, she discovered guitar and spent a good chunk of her teenage years writing stories about rock stars, while dreaming of becoming one.

Nowadays, she reads and writes in three languages, and mostly focuses on writing horror. Her first short story "The Letter" was published in *SPINE Magazine* in October 2020.

Her story "The Christmas Eve" is included in the *Bitter Chills* anthology by Blood Rites Horror.

To stay tuned with Carmilla, make sure to follow her on Instagram **@la_carmilla_**.

JOE
CLEMENTS

A varied and adaptable writer, Joe Clements made his first splash in the world of literature in *Flash Fiction Magazine* with his intense psychological short, 'Modern Medicine'. Since then he has developed several fictional universes, one of which playing host to his condensed sci-fi epic, *System Reset.*

Clements' dynamic and versatile style is influenced by everything from classic literature and poetry to films, music and even a deep interest in neuroscience and philosophy. A man of emotion, he is eager to invoke a plethora of such within the bleak, extreme and disconcerting.

MARCUS HAWKE

Marcus Hawke is a writer primarily of horror and dark fiction, some fantasy and sci-fi, and a few things that defy categorization. He was born in Toronto, moved around quite a bit during the dreaded formative years, and finally settled in Calgary where he studied at the Alberta College of Art and Design.

Many moons before that, he had aspirations of becoming a filmmaker and . . . well . . . long story short, that didn't happen. But one thing that wasn't curtailed in that time was his love for stories and the written word. Starting with the likes of R.L. Stine in childhood, it grew into a full-fledged possession thanks to the works of Stephen King, J.R.R. Tolkien, Anne Rice, and H.P. Lovecraft. A possession which, ironically, is only exorcised by succumbing to it. So here we are.

After years' worth of rejections, he finally had a short story called "Bump in the Night" published in *Jitter* magazine in 2016. Since then his work has appeared in a number of publications from Blood Rites Horror, Jitter Press, Lunatics Magazine, and most recently his first full-length novel, *The Miracle Sin*. He lives with his feline overlord in an apartment building haunted by the type of neighbours that make a person wish a ghost would come to visit in the cold, often-gloomy great white North.

In his spare time he reads, draws, paints, plays *Dungeons & Dragons*, and rambles in third person while writing bios.

www.marcushawke.com
Instagram: **@marcushawke**
Facebook: **facebook.com/MarcusHawkeAuthor**
Redbubble: **redbubble.com/MarcusHawkeShop**

PATRICK WHITEHURST

Patrick Whitehurst is a fiction and nonfiction writer. He's the author of the novellas *Monterey Noir* and *Monterey Pulp*. His third novella, *Monterey Lies*, is in the works. His most recent nonfiction book, *Haunted Monterey County*, reveals the many ghostly locations found in the California Central Coast community. He's currently at work on a new book, *Murder & Mayhem in Tucson*.

His short fiction has been featured on the Shotgun Honey website, in the anthology *Shotgun Honey Presents: Recoil*, in *Switchblade Magazine*, and in upcoming editions of *Pulp Modern* and *Hoosier Noir*. His book reviews and author interviews can be found at *Suspense Magazine*. All of his books and short stories can be found on Amazon.com.

As a journalist in Arizona, he's covered everything from the deaths of nineteen Granite Mountain Hotshots to President Barack Obama's visit to Grand Canyon.

Patrick strives in his writing to normalize the gray areas found in everyday life. Nothing is ever black and white.

MONA
KABBANI

Mona Kabbani is a horror fan, writer, and reviewer obsessed with psychology and the human condition. She emulates the conflict between good versus bad and all of the in-between in her work while providing an entertainingly horrifying experience. She is a Lebanese immigrant living the American Dream in New York City where much of her writing is inspired. You can follow her on Instagram **@moralityinhorror** for more and sign up to her mailing list on her website, **www.moralityinhorror.com**.

ALSO AVAILABLE FROM
BLOOD RITES HORROR

BITTER CHILLS
A HORROR ANTHOLOGY
FOR THE COLD SEASON

PARASITE GODS
COSMIC HORROR FOR
CANCER RESEARCH

WILD VIOLENCE
NATURE-THEMED HORROR
IN AID OF THE WWF

WELCOME TO THE FUNHOUSE
A CARNIVAL HORROR ANTHOLOGY

PULP HARVEST
SLASHER HORROR FOR HALLOWEEN NIGHT

For more anthologies, collections, and novels, head to **bloodriteshorror.com** or follow us on Instagram **@bloodriteshorror**.

More coming through 2022 . . .

DEAD SEAS   VOLUME I

TERROR IN THE
TRENCH

AN ANTHOLOGY OF AQUATIC HORROR
EDITED BY JAY ALEXANDER

Content Warnings

Here, you will find detailed content and potential trigger warnings for the stories in this book. Please be aware that there may be spoilers below.

In all/most stories:
Graphic depictions of violence and gore, foul language, moderate to extreme threat.

In *The Burning Boy*:
Murder, prolonged threat.

In *The Wild Hunt*:
Natural death (of an elderly person), mutilation.

In *The Cold, The Grief*:
Child death, grief-related trauma, cancer.

In *My White Star*:
Sexual advances without consent, murder.

In *The Killer Snowman*:
Animal death.

In *Everyone to the Table*:
Matricide, patricide, murder of a (child) sibling.

In *Every Hunt is a Cold One*:
Injury detail, cannibalism.

In *Little Billy's Naughty Christmas*:
Injury detail, matricide, patricide, corpse mutilation, foul language, adultery, gore and depiction of a mutilated sexual organ.

In *Welcome December*:
Willing physical sacrifice.

Please note: while I have made efforts to be as informative as I can about any potential triggers, there may be things I have missed. If you see anything in this book that you think should be flagged for future readers, please reach out to me at **bloodritespublishing@gmail.com** and I'll do my best in future editions.

Printed in Poland
by Amazon Fulfillment
Poland Sp. z o.o., Wrocław

81760697R00202